**"There's only ors.
His mother."**

The infant she held in ... all her protective instincts. She couldn't just hand him over and walk away. "I'm coming with you."

"I can't sanction that," Brady said.

Still holding the baby, she left the room and went down the hall to one of the desks behind the counter. "What I do is my decision. Not yours."

She slipped into her lightweight summer hiking shoes and unlocked her bottom desk drawer. In the back of the drawer she found her Glock automatic, loaded a clip and snapped the gun in a holster onto her belt.

She stood to face him. Brady was over six feet tall, and she was only five foot seven. She had to tilt her chin to look him straight in the eyes. She wouldn't mind getting to know him better, even if it meant putting up with his arrogance.

And putting up with the way her heart raced in his presence.

USA TODAY Bestselling Author

CASSIE MILES

MIDWIFE COVER

TORONTO NEW YORK LONDON
AMSTERDAM PARIS SYDNEY HAMBURG
STOCKHOLM ATHENS TOKYO MILAN MADRID
PRAGUE WARSAW BUDAPEST AUCKLAND

To the memory of Tony Chesnar, a great guy and a great friend.
And, as always, to Rick.

Recycling programs
for this product may
not exist in your area.

ISBN-13: 978-0-373-74664-4

MIDWIFE COVER

www.Harlequin.com

Printed in U.S.A.

ABOUT THE AUTHOR

Though born in Chicago and raised in L.A., *USA TODAY* bestselling author Cassie Miles has lived in Colorado long enough to be considered a semi-native. The first home she owned was a log cabin in the mountains overlooking Elk Creek, with a thirty-mile commute to her work at the *Denver Post*.

After raising two daughters and cooking tons of macaroni and cheese for her family, Cassie is trying to be more adventurous in her culinary efforts. Ceviche, anyone? She's discovered that almost anything tastes better with wine. When she's not plotting Harlequin Intrigue books, Cassie likes to hang out at the Denver Botanical Gardens near her high-rise home.

Books by Cassie Miles

CAST OF CHARACTERS

Petra Jamison—The Colorado-based midwife is a free spirit and incurable rule breaker.

Brady Masters—An FBI agent and profiler, he has a plan for everything, until he meets Petra.

Cole McClure—After he married another mountain midwife, he transferred to the Denver office of the FBI.

Escher—Brady's informant sets them on the right path.

Consuela and Miguel—A mother and son on the run from a human trafficking ring.

Francine Kelso—The former hooker runs the Lost Lamb Ranch for unwed mothers.

Margaret Woods—The young housekeeper at Lost Lamb has a son of her own, Jeremy.

Dee—Nine months pregnant and ready to deliver, she needs Petra's help.

Stan Mancuso—An attorney based in Durango, he handles the affairs of Lost Lamb.

Dr. Smith—His alias hides his true identity as a doctor involved in nefarious practices.

Robert White—The giant handyman questions his loyalty to Lost Lamb Ranch.

Chapter One

The sooner this investigation was over with, the better. After eight months in the field, Special Agent Brady Masters had reached the end of his patience. He was more than ready to return to Quantico and had paid extra, out of his own pocket, to hitch a ride on a charter flight from Albuquerque to the Grand County Airport outside Granby, Colorado.

As he disembarked from the small plane onto the tarmac, he kept his head down. The unobstructed view from the unmanned airfield on the Grand Mesa was no doubt spectacular, especially now at sunset with the blood-red skies and the clouds traced with gold, but Brady didn't give a damn about the landscape.

He'd been here for all four seasons, from winter to spring to summer and now fall. The clear air, rugged plains and distant snow-capped peaks had ceased to astound him; his career path was back east where he was being considered for a profiler position with an elite team in the Behavioral Analysis Unit. All he needed to do right now was tie up one last loose end. Then, it was bye-bye Rocky Mountains.

Waiting outside a hangar at the end of the airstrip was Special Agent Cole McClure. They'd met before, and Brady knew enough about Cole's background to appreciate the kick-ass skills of the former undercover specialist who now worked in the Denver field office.

"Where are we headed?" Cole asked as they strode side by side toward his black SUV.

Brady handed over a piece of paper on which he'd written the address and directions given to him over the phone by an informant. "If this tip pays off, we'll need backup from local law enforcement."

"Not a problem." Cole opened the car door and got behind the steering wheel. "I know the locals. My wife used to live around here. She delivered a baby for one of the deputies."

Brady fastened his seat belt. "Is your wife a doctor?"

"A midwife."

"You have a baby of your own, right?"

"Emily." As soon as he spoke his daughter's name, Cole transformed from a hard-edged federal agent into a fuzzy teddy bear with a badge.

"She's ten months old. A beauty like her mom, and she's almost walking."

"And talking?"

"She says dada." He cleared his throat and wiped the goofy grin off his face, returning his focus to FBI business. "What's our plan here? Brief me."

"As you know, I'm part of the ITEP task force."

"Illegal Transport and Exploitation of Persons," Cole said, spelling out the acronym. "I've heard that your team has had some success."

"Not enough."

They were investigating an interlinked human trafficking operation that had spread like a virus across the southwestern states from San Diego to Salt Lake City to Dallas. Even though the task force had arrested several individuals, they were playing a game of Whack-a-Mole. Each time they nabbed one, two more popped up.

"How did you get this assignment?" Cole asked.

"I'm a profiler and psychologist, specializing in interrogation. It's my job to get these guys to talk. The problem is that most of them don't know much. They're little more than delivery boys who happen to be transporting human cargo. In their minds, this is just a job."

Brady was sick of hearing their excuses, disgusted by their unintended cruelty and their indignation when they were arrested. These delivery boys weren't psychopaths, but they lacked empathy and basic decency. While they did their "jobs," they managed to ignore the fact that eighty percent of their cargo were women and children who would be processed into lives of forced labor, servitude, prostitution and worse.

"The lead we're following," Brady continued, "comes from a guy by the name of Escher who seems to have grown a conscience. He gave me a location that's used as a dropoff point—an abandoned house with a three-car garage. The property belongs to his eighty-nine-year-old grandma who doesn't live there anymore."

Cole steered the SUV onto a two-lane road leading into the hills covered with pine forests and gold-leafed aspen. "Over the river and through the woods to grandmother's house we go."

"Spoken like the father of a ten-month-old."

"What about you, Brady? Married?"

"Not yet."

"But you're looking?"

He shrugged. He didn't like to think of himself as a stubborn bachelor who was wedded to his career, but with each passing year, that identity was becoming more solidly fixed. "My twin sister says that if I don't get married soon, I'll turn into an obsessive-compulsive old fart who spends his days organizing his sock drawer and alphabetizing his canned goods."

Her analysis wasn't all that far-fetched. He had, on occasion, wondered if pinto beans should be filed under *P* for pinto or *B* for bean.

"You're a twin?"

"My sister is an agent, too. Based in Manhattan, married with one kid. She works cybercrimes."

"Do you look alike?"

"You tell me."

Brady pulled out his cell phone and flipped to a photo of himself and Barbara taken a few months ago on their thirty-second birthday. Their coloring was similar with dark blond hair and gray eyes. They both had high foreheads and square jaws, but the resemblance ended there. Nobody had ever called Brady cute, but that word perfectly described Barbara's huge smile, button nose and twinkly eyes. In the photo, she was tossing her head, laughing.

Cole said, "She's a lot prettier than you."

"As it should be." He tucked the phone back into his pocket. "How much farther?"

"According to the numbers on the mailboxes by the road, we're getting close. Maybe a mile or so."

"Are you wearing a vest?"

"Nope. Are you?"

"I am." He'd spent extra for a brand of lightweight, concealable body armor developed by the Israelis. In the field, Brady always wore a protective vest under his button-down white shirt and black suit coat. Those were the rules. "We can stop if you want to get into gear."

Cole shrugged. "I'll take my chances."

An interesting choice, Brady thought. Even though Cole had settled down and was a proud papa, he still exhibited the risk-taking behavior of an undercover operative. People could modify their behavior, but few really changed.

The road meandered through a forest that was sparsely settled with what looked like summer vacation cabins. This was a good area for a hideout—close enough to main roads for a quick getaway and secluded enough to be off the radar.

Cole turned left at a nearly indecipherable street marker for Wigwam Way. The house nearest to the corner was a quaint barn that had been remodeled into a house with a large window where the hayloft would have been. On the opposite side was a cheerful log structure with red shutters, plastic flowers in window boxes and a burned wood sign that said Welcome to the Peterson Place.

A hundred yards down the road, the charm faded as quickly as the dusk that spread shadows across the land. Scratchy letters on a rusted mailbox spelled out Escher, the name of his informant. Inside a four-foot-tall chain-link fence was a ramshackle bungalow. At one time, this little house might have been pretty, but the stucco was cracked, weathered and filthy. Weeds reached as high as the windows, many of which were busted. The gate across the driveway hung open as though someone had left in a hurry.

"That's the address." Cole drove past without stopping. "How do you want to proceed?"

"The front door was ajar. The place could be abandoned."

Brady was disappointed that they weren't closing in on suspects, but he wasn't surprised. The phone call from Escher had been hasty. His tone was angry but frightened; he was about to bolt.

At a wide spot in the road, Cole turned the SUV around. "I didn't see any vehicles, but there was the big garage."

"Like my informant said."

The three-car garage, a cheap prefab with vinyl siding, would make a good holding pen for human cargo. If there were prisoners, there would also be armed-and-dangerous guards.

Brady considered calling for backup before entering. In a city, he would have done so, but organizing a police presence in the mountains took a hell of a lot more time and effort. He wanted to get this loose end tied up and head back to Quantico.

He drew his Beretta and checked the clip. "Pull up to the front door. We'll search the house first."

"You got it."

Cole drove back, whipped down the driveway

and slammed on the brake. Brady was out of the car as soon as it stopped moving. Gun in hand, he charged toward the open door. The interior of the house was dark and dirty. A torn bedsheet hung from the curtain rod across the front window. Tattered furniture crouched on an olive green carpet. Fast food wrappers littered a coffee table along with the remains of fried chicken in a bucket. The still-greasy chicken showed that someone had been here recently.

Brady entered a narrow hallway with a bedroom at each end and a bathroom in the middle. In the front bedroom, he found a bare mattress and ragged blankets. The closet held a pile of stained clothing, both men's and women's.

The grime in the bathroom defied description.

The second bedroom had yellowed newspapers duct-taped over some of the windows. On the floor was a body, sprawled on his back with both arms thrown over his head and one leg doubled under him in a grotesque, horizontal pirouette.

Brady turned on the overhead light and called to Cole. "In here."

There was no point in feeling for a pulse. Half the man's head had been blown away. Brain matter spattered the peeling gray wallpaper, and blood puddled on the hardwood floor. Brady hunkered down beside the dead man.

Cole entered the bedroom. "Oh, man, that stinks."

"Rigor hasn't set in. He hasn't been dead for long." Brady breathed through his mouth, not wanting to inhale the stench. He pushed the body onto his side and took the wallet from the back pocket of his baggy jeans. In the cracked leatherette wallet were two fives and a driver's license. "It's Escher. My informant."

"When did he contact you?"

Brady checked his wristwatch. "Three and a half hours ago. He called me in Albuquerque."

"He might have already been here, chowing down on a bucket of chicken."

And preparing to die. Brady stood and turned away from the body. He'd only questioned Escher face-to-face once. There wasn't enough evidence to arrest him, but Brady was sure that the informant had been a coyote for many years, charging exorbitant amounts of money to smuggle illegals across the border from Mexico. That was bad enough, but nowhere near as vicious as the exploitation involved in trafficking where the human cargo was never set free. In two subsequent phone calls, Brady had played on Escher's sympathies.

Brady wondered aloud, "Why did he call me? Something must have sparked his conscience. But what?"

"Do I need to contact the Denver field office to handle forensics on the body?" Cole asked.

"We can leave the murder investigation to the local sheriff." The people who had killed Escher were already down the road. Why had the informant called? Why did he want Brady to come to this place? "Let's take a look in the garage."

He picked his way through the crap scattered throughout the little house. Looking for evidence, he'd have to paw through this garbage. There wasn't enough hand sanitizer in the world to make this right.

Outside, he sucked down a breath of fresh air. Even though he didn't expect to find anything in the garage, both he and Cole held their guns at the ready. He went to a door on the side. There were two padlocks, but the door was standing open.

As he stepped inside, he hoped with all his heart that they wouldn't find any other victims. He flicked a switch by the door. Light from two bare bulbs showed the detritus of former inhabitants. Clutter and rags. A couple of cardboard boxes. Bare mattresses. Sleeping bags. The stink of urine and sweat was overpowering.

Cole grumbled, "This must be what hell looks like."

"It's the end of the road for my investigation," Brady said. "Escher was my last viable lead."

He heard a rustling noise coming from the far

corner. Raccoons? Rats? Brady moved toward the sound. He looked down into a cardboard box. Inside, swaddled in filthy yellow blanket decorated with sheep, was an infant with round cheeks and a tiny rosebud mouth. This was what Escher had wanted him to find.

The little arms reached toward him, and Brady scooped the baby from the makeshift nest. He snuggled the tiny bundle against his chest. "How old do you think it is?"

"Not more than a couple of weeks," Cole said.

"You sure?"

"Pretty much. With my wife's job, I'm around babies a lot." He reached out and stroked the fine black hair on the infant's head. "Doesn't seem to be injured, but we should check it out. I know where to take this little one."

The baby wriggled. The mouth suckled an invisible teat. Brady had nothing to feed this infant. All he could offer was a promise that he would point the abandoned child toward a better life.

Trafficking in newborns was a new and horrible twist in the ITEP investigation—something he couldn't ignore. Brady knew he wouldn't be returning to Quantico today.

Chapter Two

In the front reception area of the Rocky Mountain Women's Clinic in Granby, Petra Jamison stood on her head with her elbows forming a tripod and her bare feet against the wall for support. She'd propped the front doors open to allow the early evening breezes to waft inside and dispel the faintly antiseptic smell from the examination rooms. In about an hour, a group of pregnant women would arrive for Petra's class on prenatal yoga breathing, and she'd decided to get in the mood by playing a CD of Navajo wooden flute music and doing meditation exercises.

Even though the room was dimly lit with only one lamp on the desk behind the counter and a three-wick sandalwood candle on the coffee table, she was bathed in the warm glow of positivity. Her mind and body were in balance. The rush of blood to her brain gave her a burst of energy at the end of the day. As if she needed an evening wake-up. Petra had the circadian rhythm of a night owl, maybe because she was born at midnight. Or maybe her preference for the dark had something to do with her fair complexion— people who freckle shouldn't go out in the sun. Or maybe...

She heard a vehicle pull into the parking lot. A car door slammed. Still upside down, she saw a man in a black suit and white shirt holding a baby in his arms. He strode toward her and leaned over, tilting his head to squint into her face. He had tense eyes and the kind of high forehead that she associated with intelligence, even though she knew hairline was nothing more than a geneti- cally determined growth pattern. Was he smart? Or clever? Did he have a sense of humor? Prob- ably not. This guy didn't look like Mr. Giggle.

"Back up," she said.

"What?"

"I need for you to back up so I can put my legs down."

When he stepped backward, the baby started crying.

Petra lowered her legs, stood and adjusted the long, auburn braid that hung down her back. Before she could say anything, Cole McClure charged into the reception area.

"Hey, lady," Cole greeted her. "I need your help."

"Anything for you." She liked Cole, even though

her fellow midwife and friend, Rachel, had moved away from Granby when she married him. "How's little Emily?"

"Perfect." He made the introduction. "Petra Jamison, midwife, meet Brady Masters, special agent."

"Hi, Brady." She purposely used his first name instead of his title. The clinic was her space, and her protocol applied. In here, it didn't matter if you were a bank president or a car mechanic—she'd delivered babies for women with both of those occupations. "May I take the baby?"

"Be my guest."

When he transferred the tiny bundle into her arms, her fingers brushed against his chest. It was hard as a rock. "Are you wearing Kevlar?"

"It's a protective vest."

She glanced between the two men. Even though Cole had on a dark blazer, his jeans and blue shirt were casual. Quite the opposite, Brady matched the stereotype for men in black, right down to his body armor. His underpants were probably government-issue. "Do you mind telling me why this baby has an FBI escort?"

"Long story," Brady said.

The poor thing was filthy, swaddled in a blanket with a sheep design. The baby's cries were fitful. The little face twisted in a knot.

She blew out the candle and went down the hallway that was covered with hundreds of photos of families who had used the clinic over the past five years.

In a spacious lavender room with sinks, cabinets and a refrigerator, she placed the wailing infant on a changing table and removed the blanket. There was a logo in the corner and a blood stain, but she saw no wounds on the baby as she peeled off a grungy T-shirt and a cloth diaper that looked like it hadn't been changed in a very long time. "When's the last time this little boy ate anything?"

"Don't know," Brady said.

She shoved the discarded clothing and blanket aside. "You probably need those things for evidence. Trash bags are in that cabinet. Cole, would you prepare a bottle of formula? You know where everything is."

While the two feds did her bidding, she slid a portable tub into one side of the double sink. Using a soft cloth, she gave the baby a quick wash, inspecting him for cuts and rashes. The warm water soothed his cries until he was only emitting an occasional hiccup.

"Is he okay?" Brady asked.

"I think he's going to be just fine," she said. "Nothing wrong with his lungs, that's for sure."

After she dried him off, she applied a medicinal salve to his chafed bottom, put on a biodegradable diaper and swaddled him in a clean white blanket. She took the bottle from Cole and teased the nipple into the baby boy's mouth. After only a few tries, he started sucking.

The whole process had taken less than ten minutes; Petra was an expert. She looked toward Cole who was on his cell phone. Even though she didn't really want to talk to Special Agent Brady, she spoke to him in a soft voice that wouldn't upset the feeding infant. "I'd like an explanation."

"Nothing you need to worry about," he said. "Thanks for taking care of the, um, immediate problem."

"Are you referring to the poopy diaper?"

He scowled as though it was below him to discuss poop. This guy was uber-intense. Tight-lipped, he said, "The infant needs to be turned over to Child Protective Services."

"There's only one thing this baby needs. His mother. What happened to her? Is she dead?"

"Why would you think—"

"There was blood on the blanket. A big smear right next to the logo for Lost Lamb Ranch, whatever that is. So, what happened? Did you find the baby at a crime scene?"

Even though Brady had already washed his hands, he used a spritz of hand sanitizer. "The short answer is yes. There was a crime. We don't know where the mother is."

"I might be able to help. I don't know all the pregnant women in the area, but I've got a pretty good network. Should I ask around?"

"That won't be necessary." His gray eyes were cool and distant. "We have reason to believe the mother isn't from around here."

"On the run?" she guessed.

His expression gave nothing away.

"Is she a hostage? Or kidnapped?"

"It's an ongoing investigation. I can't discuss it. You understand."

She took his condescending attitude as a challenge to figure out what was going on. The infant she held in her arms had switched on all her protective instincts. She couldn't just hand him over and walk away.

"It must have been something terrible," she said, "that separated the mother from her baby. In spite of how dirty he was, he'd been taken care of. Mom didn't want to abandon him."

Brady said nothing.

She could only think of two reasons a mother would leave her baby behind. "Either she was forced to run or she thought the baby would be safer without her. If I had to guess, I'd say that mother and baby were being transported illegally."

"Good guess," Cole said as he ended his phone call. "I checked in with the sheriff, and he put me through to one of his deputies who picked up an injured woman—an illegal with no green card. She kept saying that her baby was stolen."

"How badly is she injured?" Brady asked.

"Knife wounds. A lot of blood," Cole reported. "The deputy took her to Doc Wilson's house. It was closer to his location than any hospital or clinic. The doc stitched her up. He says she'll be fine."

"We need to talk to her," Brady said.

"I told the deputy to stay with her at the doc's place. If anybody is after her, she could be in danger."

Petra listened with rising concern as they discussed their plan to drive to Doc Wilson's place. Her heart went out to this mother. She wanted to help. "I'm coming with you."

"I can't sanction that," Brady said.

Still holding the baby, she left the room and went down the hall to one of the desks behind the counter. "What I do is my decision. Not yours."

"You heard what Cole said. It's dangerous."

She whipped around and transferred the baby into Brady's arms. "Keep the nipple in his mouth. He needs to get as much hydration and nourishment as possible."

Sitting in her ergonomic desk chair, she slipped into her lightweight summer hiking shoes and unlocked her bottom desk drawer. In the back of the drawer, she found her GLOCK automatic, loaded a clip into the magazine and snapped the gun in a holster onto her belt.

"No," Brady said firmly. "You're a civilian."

She pointed to a yellow-painted brick that she was using as a paperweight. "You know what that is?"

"An award for completing the Yellow Brick Road at Quantico."

She gave a nod to her former career path as an FBI special agent. "I was number one on the obstacle course back then, and I've kept up my skills. Besides, I can take care of the baby."

"The baby? Who said anything about taking the baby?"

She stood to face him. Brady was over six feet tall, and she was only five feet, seven inches. She had to tilt her chin to look him straight in the eyes. "If you want the mom to talk, you need the baby. She's not going to open her mouth when she's in a panic about her missing child."

For a full twenty seconds, he glared at her, definitely ticked off. Then he inhaled deeply, exhaled and conceded. "You're right."

"Wow, I didn't expect you to give in."

"You might have the wrong impression of me."

"Let's see." She took a step back and looked him up and down. "My first impression is that you're rigid, controlling and always follow the rules. Pretty much the opposite of me. Is that about right?"

"Not bad for a superficial description."

"Could you do better? Go on, tell me about myself."

"You don't want to play this game."

Another challenge? She couldn't let it pass. "I insist. Tell me your impression of me."

"A risk-taker," he said in a low voice meant only for her ears. "Pretty much fearless, but you're afraid of fire."

"What?" How had he known that?

"You heard me," Brady said. "You come from a family where at least one member is in law enforcement. You're rebellious and always root for the underdog. You're honest to the point of tactless. You say that you don't care what other people think but you're sensitive. You lost someone close to you—a boyfriend or a fiancé. And you're from northern California, near San Francisco."

Taken aback, she gaped. He'd been correct on every single count. "Either you're a psychic or a damn good profiler."

"Psychics don't generally become special agents," he said. "If you come with us to pick up the mother, I'm going to insist that you wear a protective vest."

"Fine."

His snap analysis intrigued her. She wouldn't

mind getting to know him better, even if it meant putting up with his arrogance.

BRADY DECIDED THEY SHOULD take two vehicles. Cole had already left in Petra's truck and would coordinate backup with other officers from the sheriff's department. Brady, Petra and the baby would ride together in the black SUV. His plan was to pick up the witness and take her into FBI custody. He'd already put in a call for a chopper to meet them at the airfield.

Through the windshield of the SUV, he watched as she stood on the sidewalk talking to four hugely pregnant women. The ladies waddled into the clinic, and Petra came toward him with the baby in her arms. Over her left shoulder, she carried a diaper bag filled with supplies. Her right hand was free to draw the GLOCK automatic from the side holster that was only partially hidden under her long purple vest.

A gun-toting midwife wasn't his first choice as a partner, but he could work with Petra. She was FBI-trained and would do anything to protect the baby. Her instinct to reunite the mother with her child had been smart.

She arranged the sleeping baby in the carrier she'd installed in the back of the SUV. Safety first. He approved.

When she opened the door to the passenger

side, he held out the dark blue Kevlar vest with FBI stenciled across the back. It wasn't necessary for him to repeat his order; she knew what needed to be done.

As she donned the protective armor, her blue eyes expressed an irony that contrasted the sweetness of her full lips and the innocence of the freckles that spread across her cheeks. She reminded him of a mischievous kid, but he wouldn't make the mistake of thinking she was immature.

She hopped into the seat and fastened her seat belt across the vest. "Happy?"

"Delirious."

He pulled away from the curb. The GPS in the dashboard showed him the route to Doc Wilson's address, which seemed simple enough. Five miles outside town, he'd turn left on Conifer Street, then another three miles on a winding road. "Tell me what kind of cover we'll find at Doc Wilson's house."

"Are you expecting an ambush?"

"I want to be prepared for any possibility."

"It's a two-story log cabin in a forested area. There's a small clinic with a parking lot attached to the right side of the house. Doc's retired but still sees a few patients."

The forest bothered him. If the traffickers had picked up the deputy's scent, they could sneak into Doc's clinic without being seen. He remembered the brutally murdered body of his informant sprawled on the floor. These were vicious men who had reason to silence the witness.

"Fill me in," she said. "What are we looking for?"

"Your job is to take care of the baby and the mother. That's it. Period. Nothing else."

"I should question her," Petra said. "I mean, look at you and look at me. A terrified woman who almost lost her son is way more likely to open up to another woman. Plus, she's an illegal, and I speak Spanish. Do you?"

"Fluently." Once again, she'd outlined a good plan. A woman-to-woman conversation would probably be more productive than an interrogation. "We'll both question her. I'm looking for the obvious information. Names, places and dates."

"Was she brought here by a coyote? I hate those guys." She shuddered with anger. The wisps of red hair that had escaped her braid flared around her face like flames. "What they do is so wrong on so many levels."

For a moment, Brady considered telling her about the ITEP investigation into human trafficking and the sickening possibility that infants were being drawn into this web of crime. Her righteous rage matched his own feelings about the victimization of helpless people. This was a passionate woman, perhaps too much so. Her emotions were close to the surface.

He decided against adding fuel to her fire. "Our focus is to get information that can be acted upon immediately."

"So we want to talk to her right away."

"Correct." Time was of the essence. The traffickers might still be in the area, and he needed to find them.

The light from a half moon and a sky filled with stars illuminated the sparsely populated land beyond the city borders. There were only a couple of houses with lights in the windows and few headlights on the two-lane road.

He used his hands-free phone to contact Cole. "Are you there yet?"

"Just approaching the house," Cole said. "I haven't seen any sign of the other deputies."

"Don't go in alone. Wait for me."

"We might have a problem," Cole said. "A few minutes ago, the deputy at Doc's called me. Even though I could hear the woman sobbing and yelling in the background, he said he had everything under control and didn't need my help. He said he'd meet me at the sheriff's department."

"He was warning you off."

"That's what I thought," Cole said, "but I played along and asked him if he was sure he didn't need assistance."

"His answer?"

"He confirmed that he didn't need help. I could barely make out what the woman was saying. It sounded like she said, 'Don't hurt my baby.'"

Brady feared that the traffickers had caught up to the witness at Doc's place. He might be headed into danger. Worse than that, he'd dragged Petra and the baby along with him.

Chapter Three

In the reflected light from the dashboard, Petra studied Brady's profile as he ended his call. Intuitively, she knew something was bothering him. Not that he'd been cheerful before, but he was definitely darker and more serious.

"What's wrong?" she asked.

"When I exit the vehicle, you get into the driver's seat. If I don't signal you in five minutes, drive away fast. Do not, I repeat, do not enter the house."

"I'm armed," she reminded him.

Under his breath, he said, "Please don't kill anybody."

"I'm just saying… If there's a threat, I can respond."

"A dead suspect isn't going to do me much good. I need for you to concentrate on one thing—keeping the baby safe."

She didn't argue. It didn't take FBI training for her to realize that there needed to be one clear leader in a crisis situation. "Are you going to wait for Cole?"

"He's already at the house." Brady eased up on the accelerator and drove slowly past a black panel van parked at the side of the road.

"What is it?" she asked.

"California plates on that van."

Tension prickled along the surface of her skin. She rested her hand on the butt of her weapon. When she'd made her bold pronouncement about keeping up her skills, she hadn't really expected to fire the GLOCK. And target practice was a lot different than facing real danger. "Do you think the van belongs to your suspect?"

His fingers tensed on the steering wheel. "How far are we from Doc's place?"

"I'm not sure." This narrow, winding road followed a small creek, and one curve looked much like another. "I think it's just around the next bend."

He was still driving slowly. His headlights slashed through the trunks of pine trees into the forest. She caught a glimpse of something moving and pointed. "There."

Gunfire rang out. Three shots. The windshield cracked.

Brady hit the brakes. Petra tore off her seat belt and ducked. From the backseat, the baby jolted awake and started wailing.

"Drive away," Brady shouted as he jumped from the car.

He ran into the forest, charging directly into harm's way. His white shirt contrasted with the trees and the brush at the edge of the road. His black suit faded into the night, but that gleaming shirt was a target for the gunman.

She wanted to go after him and provide the kind of backup he'd need in facing an armed-and-dangerous suspect. But her first concern was protecting the infant.

Petra scrambled over the center console and got behind the wheel. There were two bullet holes in the windshield. The shooter hadn't been kidding around. He wanted them dead.

More gunshots split the air. She heard a high-pitched scream. Where was Cole? Where were the other deputies?

There wasn't room on the road to turn around, so she flipped the SUV into Reverse. As she backed up, her headlights lit up the scene that played out in front of her. She braked to a stop and took her gun from the holster.

Brady was facing a gunman who held a woman carelessly around her waist. Her hands were fastened behind her back, and she was yelling in Spanish. *Ayudame*. Help me.

Both men dodged behind tree trunks. Even though Brady was returning gunfire shot for shot, she knew he wasn't taking aim. He wouldn't risk hitting the hostage. Nor would she.

But Petra might provide a distraction. She buzzed down her window and fired her weapon into the air.

The gunman swung toward her. With his arm outstretched, he aimed at the SUV and fired. Bullets smacked against the hood. In the backseat behind her, the baby continued to cry.

She ducked, barely peeking over the dashboard, and she saw Brady make his move. With one running step, he mounted a rock that was the size of an ottoman. Using that height, he launched himself through the air toward the gunman. It was the boldest, bravest, stupidest thing she'd ever seen in her life. But it worked. Brady knocked the gunman off his feet.

Her breath caught in her throat. The two men struggled on the ground amid the brush. She couldn't tell what was happening. Desperately, she wanted to help, to leave the SUV and go to Brady's aid.

Another vehicle rumbled toward her. She recognized her truck. Cole was coming back toward them from Doc's house.

In the glow of her headlights, she saw Brady stagger to his feet. He held the woman against his chest. His gun was aimed at the suspect on the ground.

Relief washed through her. And pride. Brady might think of himself as someone who would never break the rules, but she was pretty sure that his diving leap at an armed suspect wasn't standard FBI procedure. He'd taken a risk, a big one.

She wriggled in her seat, wanting to rush toward him. But she knew the protocol. Until she was one-hundred-percent sure it was safe, she needed to stay in the car with the baby whose cries had faded to a whimper.

With gun drawn, Cole went toward Brady and the woman. They talked for a moment. Cole took custody of the suspect on the ground. Brady freed the ties that bound the woman's hands behind her back and helped her toward the SUV.

Leaning on Brady's arm, the dark-haired woman limped forward. She had bandages on both forearms. Her clothes were spattered with blood, bruises marred her face and her long dark hair hung in a tangled mass. Still, she dragged herself toward her baby.

Petra got out of the SUV and opened the back door. In seconds, she freed the baby from the carrier. Holding the tiny bundle, she went toward Brady and the mother whose arms were raised, reaching desperately.

When Petra handed her the child, the woman gasped. She sank to her knees on the ground, cradling her infant to her breast. She rocked back and forth, holding him and quietly sobbing.

Before Petra could compliment Brady on his rescue, he said, "She told me there were only two men. The guy in custody and Escher who we already know is dead. Ask her again. I need to be sure."

Petra hunkered down beside the woman. "He's all right. Your baby is all right."

Her exhausted eyes sought Petra's face. *"Mijo es bueno."*

"Si, muy bueno." She smiled and gently rested her hand on the woman's trembling shoulders. "What's his name? *¿Cómo se llamo?*"

"Miguel."

"And your name?"

"Consuela."

In Spanish, Petra asked if there were any other bad guys. Consuela replied that there were only the two, and Escher wasn't a bad man. He had tried to help her and to save Miguel.

Petra rose and faced Brady. "She says it was just the two of them."

"I'll take her word for it."

She heard police sirens approaching and glanced toward Cole. He had the suspect sitting on the ground with his hands cuffed behind his back. "What about Doc and the deputy? Are they okay?"

"Cole entered the clinic and found them both tied up. The deputy had been knocked unconscious. Doc is taking care of him."

"I'm surprised this guy didn't kill them."

"He's not stupid enough to kill a deputy."

Through the trees, she saw the red and blue lights of an approaching ambulance and a police vehicle. As soon as they all arrived, regular police procedure would take over, and she'd be shunted out of the way.

She'd probably never see Brady Masters again, which shouldn't have bothered her. The uptight fed wasn't her type. If they spent more time in each other's company, they'd surely drive each other crazy. Still, she felt a twinge of regret…and a bit of curiosity.

"I have a question, Brady. How did you know I'm afraid of fire?"

"Are you asking me to give away my profiler secrets?"

"I am."

He took her elbow and pulled her aside, creating a bubble of privacy as the ambulance parked. He leaned close. His gaze rested gently on her face, and his voice was just above a whisper as he confided, "When we were at the clinic, you blew out the candle before you left the room. Since you're a rule-breaker, that precaution seemed out of character, unless you have a fear of fire."

"Very observant." When she smiled at him, he did the same, and she noticed a dimple on the left side of his mouth. "And how did you know I'm from San Francisco?"

"That was easy. There's a beat-up orange-and-black Giants baseball cap on the file cabinet nearest your desk."

"Of course," she said. "I wear it so often I don't even notice it anymore."

"I noticed a lot about you, Petra." As an SUV with the Grand County sheriff's logo on the side parked behind the ambulance, he stepped away from her. "I might need to contact you again. I have some questions of my own."

"You know where to find me."

He strode toward the other officers and the paramedics who were helping the mother and baby. Immediately, Brady took charge, issuing orders that nobody seemed to question.

She wondered if they'd meet again. They seemed to connect on some level. Would he contact her?

She hoped so.

FOUR DAYS LATER, IT WAS Petra's day off, and she was still in bed at half past ten. She didn't want to get up and end a marathon of dreams about Brady.

Dreams were important to her. Whether they represented fears that bubbled up from the unconscious or were prescient whisperings from magical beings, dreams had a meaning. Why had Brady become the star player in her nighttime dramas? She rolled onto her back, kicked off the forest green comforter and stared up at the ceiling as she considered.

Most of her Brady dreams were as obvious as a twelve-foot-tall neon sign. They involved kissing and caressing and Brady with his necktie hanging loose and his white shirt unbuttoned. His chest heaved with desire as he stalked toward her, grabbed her and dominated her. Oh, yeah, she knew exactly what those dreams were telling her. *I need a lover.*

The last time she had a serious boyfriend was almost a year ago which wasn't surprising because, as a rule, midwives don't come into contact with a lot of eligible men. Any halfway decent guy—even an arrogant, obsessively neat fed—was enough to get her motor revving.

But these weren't all sexy dreams. In another, she saw him with a baby in his arms. That was how they met, and she might be replaying that moment. But was there another interpretation? Something about fertility? She was twenty-nine and not getting any younger. Because Brady appeared to be a fine healthy sperm donor, he might represent her desire to have a baby of her own.

An old, familiar ache tightened around her

heart. Her chances of conceiving a baby were slim to none. Those dreams were unlikely to come true.

She dragged herself out of bed and padded barefoot down the hall to the kitchen where she got the coffeemaker started. Yesterday, she'd been with a mom who was in labor for six hours before she delivered a gorgeous baby girl, seven pounds, six ounces. Petra felt the need to stretch her legs. This would be a good day for a run.

After she washed up and pulled her hair into a high ponytail, she slipped into a pair of shorts and a yellow-and-red Bob Marley T-shirt. With her coffee mug in hand, she went out the back door onto the patio behind the two-bedroom, frame house she was renting. The morning sun warmed her face as she sat on top of the redwood picnic table with her running shoes on the attached bench. From this vantage point, she surveyed the remnants of her vegetable garden. In spite of the early frost in August, she still had zucchini.

Maybe she'd bake zucchini bread and take a loaf to the parents of the new baby. They were a terrific couple, and she had no doubt that this was another family where she'd always be welcomed as Aunt Petra. That kind of friendship was a satisfying feeling, a great feeling. But was it really what she wanted in life?

Staring into her coffee mug, she wondered. She

loved being a midwife and appreciated the simple pleasures of baking and gardening, but the action-packed hour she'd spent with Brady reminded her of her time at Quantico. While training to be an FBI agent, she'd scored high on marksmanship, kicked ass on the Yellow Brick Road obstacle course and was at the head of her class. She missed the adrenaline rush.

"Petra?"

She turned her head and saw him. "Brady, where did you come from?"

"I've been knocking on your front door."

He sauntered around the corner of her house and stepped onto the patio. His cargo pants and black T-shirt made a very different impression from the first time she met him—so different that she wasn't sure he was real. This version of Brady was more like the sexy guy she'd been dreaming about. He looked fit and strong. His uncombed hair seemed to be a lighter shade of blond. He had a few days' growth of stubble on his chin.

This version of Brady was hot, hot, hot. Looking at him made her heart pump faster. It took an effort to keep the mug from trembling in her hands. "Would you like some coffee?"

"If it's not too much trouble."

She climbed off the picnic table and went through the back door into the kitchen. For Brady's coffee, she chose a handmade mug with a blue-

and-green glaze. She turned toward him. "Cream or sugar?"

"I take my coffee plain and hot."

"Like your women?" She'd blurted the comment without thinking. "Sorry, I didn't mean to be inappropriate. It's just that you look different without your black suit."

"I'm going undercover."

She poured his coffee and handed the mug to him. "That's not a typical assignment for a profiler."

"It's only my second time," he said as he took his coffee to the small table in the kitchen and sat. "One of the reasons I came here was to tell you what happened to Consuela and Miguel. You deserve to know."

"I appreciate that." She'd been worried about the mother and baby.

"You understand that this is FBI business, and you can't talk about it."

"Yes, sir." She gave him a mocking salute.

"Consuela's story started in Mexico. She wanted to be with her husband for the birth of their first child, and she paid a coyote to take her to where her husband was working on a construction crew outside Las Vegas. She never got there. Instead, she fell into the hands of a human trafficking gang."

She winced as though she'd been slapped.

Human trafficking was the modern equivalent of slavery. These people were used and abused until the marrow had been sucked from their bones and there was nothing left. When death came, it was a mercy. "That's what you've been investigating."

"The FBI has a task force in the field. I've been working with them for eight months. I thought I was done, but I've got to follow up on what I learned from Consuela."

Petra sat at the small table opposite Brady. "What did she tell you?"

"She gave birth to Miguel in the back of a semi. The other women helped her, and they managed to keep the baby a secret for a while. Two of them were also pregnant."

"I thought most girls picked up by traffickers were forced into prostitution. Pregnant women wouldn't do them much good." The truth hit her. "Oh, my God, they want the babies."

He gave a terse nod. "One of the men in charge of Consuela's group figured that out. His name was Escher. He'd been a coyote for years, but the idea of stealing babies and dumping them into a horrible and uncertain future was too much, even for him. He called me."

"He was your informant."

"Consuela said that he tried to free them all. He didn't really think they had much chance and told her to leave Miguel behind. Escher promised to protect the infant."

"By running away, she thought she was saving her son," Petra said.

"Instead, Escher was killed. His partner—the suspect we arrested—tried to find the others, but they were gone, everyone but Consuela who stayed behind to find her baby."

"And now?" she asked. "What's going to happen to Consuela and Miguel?"

"They're reunited with her husband and in protective custody. We need her testimony to convict our suspect. After that, I'm not sure what will happen with immigration. At least, their family is together. They're all healthy and safe."

It wasn't a perfect happy ending, but the fate of Consuela and Miguel wasn't as terrible as it might have been. They'd escaped. How many others wouldn't make it?

Unable to sit still, she rose from the table and paced across her kitchen to the counter where she poured herself another cup of coffee. She didn't need the caffeine. Her blood surged. She was fired up.

This type of injustice was why she'd wanted to be in the FBI. When Brady did his analysis of her, he said she always fought for the underdog. So true. "I wish there was something I could do."

"There is," he said. "I told you I was going undercover to investigate the trafficking in babies. And I could use your help."

"Anything," she said.

"Will you be my wife?"

Chapter Four

Needless to say, Brady was one-hundred-and-ten-percent serious about his investigation. Enlisting Petra's help wasn't something he took lightly. Still, he hadn't been able to resist teasing her.

Her reaction was huge. Her eyebrows flew up to her hairline. A pink flush dappled her cheeks as she gaped at him, slack-jawed. She stammered, "You w-w-w-want me to do what?"

"Be my wife." He leaned back in his chair and calmly sipped his coffee, enjoying the show. "I'm sure it's not the first time someone has asked."

"Well, no. Not that it's any of your business." She braced herself against the kitchen counter. "I need an explanation."

"Being my wife? I think you know what that means—a white picket fence, a couple of kids and a dog 'til death do us part. Love, honor and obey, especially obey…"

"I'll obey you when hell freezes over."

"We can tinker with the vows. I'm flexible."

"You can go…flex yourself." She stalked to the back door. "I'm out of here."

The screen door slammed behind her with a final sounding slap. Apparently, Petra didn't respond well to teasing. He'd known she was the sensitive type, but he hadn't expected her to get so upset. Had he accidentally pinched a nerve? She was twenty-nine years old. Marriage might be a hot-button issue.

He rose slowly from the table, disappointed that he wouldn't be seeing more of Petra Jamison but glad that he'd found out now that they couldn't work together. Damn, she was touchy. If she'd thrown a hissy while they were in the middle of their undercover assignment, the consequences would be bad.

When he stepped outside into the crisp fall sunlight, she was waiting for him with her fists stuck on her slim hips. "You said you needed my help. I want to know more."

The smart move was to keep walking, to move away from her. "This isn't your problem."

She stepped in front of him, blocking his path. "Wait up, Brady. I know you were teasing."

"Well, yeah."

"Give me another chance." She swallowed hard. "I might have overreacted."

He figured that was the closest thing to an apology he was going to get. If she could stay cool, she was the perfect person for the undercover job. He reached into one of the pockets in his cargo pants, took out a photograph and handed it to her. "Do you remember this?"

"It's the blanket that was wrapped around Miguel. With the sheep design and the blood and the logo for Lost Lamb Ranch."

"Lost Lamb Ranch was the destination for Consuela and the other pregnant women. We think it's some kind of clearing house for baby trafficking."

"Why can't the FBI just shut it down?"

"Supposedly, this ranch is a nonprofit home for unwed mothers. On paper, they look legit. They file their taxes and pay their bills. The adoptions arranged through Lost Lamb seem to fulfill all the proper requirements, but I think they're a front for trafficking. If I can get inside and find out who's really running the show, then I can shut them down, lock them up and make sure they never hurt another child."

Her head bobbed, and her ponytail bounced. "That's why you're going undercover to investigate."

"But I don't have an in."

"And I do," she said.

"What's more natural than a midwife looking for work at a facility for unwed mothers?"

"So we'll move to the area," she said, "and I'll be your undercover wife."

"Isn't that what I said?"

"Not exactly."

He didn't push the issue. The time for teasing was over. "I won't lie to you. This assignment is dangerous, and it's not your responsibility. I want you to consider before you give me your answer."

"How long would it take? I can't be away from work."

"All taken care of. Cole's wife will move up here and handle your caseload. We'll say you had a family emergency."

"Wait a minute. You've already talked this over with Cole and Rachel?"

"It was Rachel's idea for me to approach you."

He was well aware that Cole's wife had a matchmaking agenda for him and Petra. Because her marriage had turned out well, Rachel was anxious for her friend to find an FBI husband of her own.

Brady didn't bother telling her that he and Petra wouldn't make a good match. Not that he didn't find the feisty redhead attractive. He liked her careless beauty, even the freckles. And she had a killer body. But they were from different planets when it came to temperament. She was all emotion, and he was completely rational.

From the few minutes he'd spent in her kitchen, he knew she'd drive him crazy. Her home was clean but cluttered, with all kinds of scribbled kids' pictures hanging on the fridge and the countertops lined with containers were in every shape and size—ranging from clear glass to something that looked like a purple mushroom.

"Let's walk," she said.

He fell into step beside her as they went down her driveway onto the sidewalk. This was a pleasant residential neighborhood with small, frame houses on large lots. At the corner, she turned left. They were going uphill.

She asked, "Why me?"

"Obviously, there's your occupation. It's tough for an undercover operative to fake being a midwife, especially if they're asked to deliver a baby. And I've seen you in action. You don't get rattled under pressure."

"But I do get rattled," she muttered. "I don't like being teased."

"Duly noted," he said. "I also looked into your record at Quantico. You were top of your class, scored off-the-charts in all kinds of tests and were on your way to becoming an outstanding field agent."

"But I quit."

The incident that caused her to leave the FBI had been described in a Supervisory Special Agent's report along with a somewhat hostile notation about her tendency to flaunt the rules. "Tell me what happened."

"I got a message from my brother. He's a cop in San Francisco. At the time, he worked with my boyfriend who was also a cop. Everybody in my family, except my mom, has a career that involves protecting people. My sister is in the Army. My dad is an arson inspector for the San Francisco Fire Department."

Her father's occupation seemed like an explanation for her fear of fire, but her background raised other questions. How could a free spirit like Petra exist in a family that followed and enforced the rules?

Two blocks away from the end of the street where they were walking, he saw a forested area. "Tell me about your mom."

"Best cook in the world." Her mouth relaxed into a grin. "Sometimes, she worked at her father's restaurant and made the most amazing Greek food. When I was a kid, I loved to go with her, even though my yaya would always pat me on the head and say that my red hair meant trouble."

"Yaya?"

"Grandmother," she said. "She moved to the United States when she was eight and became a citizen. But she is Greek, first and always. She believed redheads were either descended directly from the gods or were wild and wanton, maybe even vampires."

"She thought you were different." Maybe a self-fulfilling prophecy for Petra. "It sounds like you preferred the more creative lifestyle at the restaurant. But you chose to join the FBI."

"All through high school and college I was kind of wild. Let's just say it didn't turn out well. I was twenty-one, and I figured it was time to give my father's way a try."

Her digression into describing her family life had given him useful insights into her personality. "You still haven't told me why you quit the FBI."

They'd reached the forest. She left the sidewalk and followed a narrow path that led into a thick grove of aspen. A brisk wind rushed through the white trunks, and the golden leaves shimmered like precious coins.

Petra wrapped her hand around one slender trunk and tilted her head back. The reflected light picked out blond highlights in her auburn hair as she returned to her story. "Like I said, my brother called. He told me that my boyfriend had been seriously injured in the line of duty, and I left Quantico without going through proper procedures."

According to the account he'd read, she wasn't cleared to leave the training area and had sneaked outside the perimeter, evading the surveillance. Then she'd flagged down a car, using her FBI credentials. After she was on a flight to San Francisco, she'd called her supervisor.

Even though Brady admired her resourcefulness, he didn't understand her refusal to go through regular channels. "You would have qualified for compassionate leave."

"I doubt it." She shrugged. "This was a boyfriend. Not a fiancé. Not a husband. I was pretty sure I'd be told to suck it up and get back to work. And I couldn't do that. I just couldn't. I had to be with him."

This was a clear example of following reckless emotion rather than logic. "Then what happened?"

"I got a stern reprimand, and it ticked me off. I quit. Flat out and permanently. I wanted nothing more to do with the FBI with all those rules and regulations." She tossed him a grin. "Here's the irony. My boyfriend recovered in just a couple of weeks. And the big, fat jerk dumped me."

"And you went to school to become a midwife."

"Which turned out to be a job I love. Maybe I ought to send the jerk a thank-you card."

Brady had a fairly good idea what he was getting into by bringing Petra into his undercover assignment—a whole lot of passion and drama. On the plus side, being undercover wasn't a stretch for her. Nobody would ever think this woman was with law enforcement.

"Think about the assignment," he said. "I need your answer as soon as possible."

She walked along the path, touching the trunk of each tree she passed. "Did you know that the druids believed the aspen was sacred? They'd come into a grove like this, sit quietly and listen to the rustling and watch the quaking leaves until they reached enlightenment."

"Didn't know that." He really didn't give a damn about druids.

"And there's a Ute legend about how the Great Spirit cursed the proud aspen. Because it refused to bow to him, the tree would forever tremble whenever anyone looked at it."

"What's your point?"

"I'm looking at the big picture." She plucked a leaf and twirled it between her fingers as she came back toward him. "My answer is yes."

"Did the tree tell you to say that?"

"I came to this decision all by myself," she said. "If it means rescuing babies, I'll do anything. I'll even pretend to be your wife."

She didn't sound particularly happy about the idea, which was fine with him. This was an investigation, not a romance.

By two o'clock in the afternoon, Petra had made her excuses to the clinic and arranged for Rachel to take over her caseload. She'd packed one suitcase with clothes and shoes. Her other odds and ends went into a couple of cardboard boxes. Altogether, her personal items took up only a few square feet in the back of her truck, which was fortunate because Brady's possessions filled the rest of the space to overflowing.

His undercover identity was as a struggling artist, and he'd brought along easels, equipment and a couple of crates of artwork. Added to those were several other unmarked cardboard boxes he'd gathered from grocery and liquor stores.

Leaning against the side of the truck, she watched as he transferred his things from the back of his minivan. He loaded not one, not two, but four cases of bottled water.

She arched a skeptical eyebrow. "I'm pretty sure they have water in Durango."

"I like this brand."

Even though she'd be first in line to promote the benefits of staying hydrated, she didn't believe the taste varied much. Water was water. "What's in all those boxes?"

"Kitchen supplies, linens, electronics. I haven't labeled anything because that's not something my undercover character would do."

"Ah, yes. You're supposed to be Brady Gilliam, former alcoholic and artist from San Francisco, who inherited a house not far from the Lost Lamb Ranch."

"And you're my wife, Patty."

She frowned. "How come you get to keep your first name and I don't?"

"Petra is an unusual name. If somebody goes

snooping around on the internet, looking for information on midwives, they might make the connection to your real identity."

He already had her documentation in hand—a fake California driver's license and social security card. Apparently, he'd been confident that she'd agree to his proposal before he'd even talked to her. Although she didn't like to think of herself as predictable, his conclusion was totally logical, given what happened the first time they'd met. She was someone who took action. And she didn't hesitate to protect the helpless.

To establish the rest of her undercover identity, Brady did a computer consultation with the FBI computer techs. They produced a dossier on Patty Gilliam's history, including a website and online presence.

She didn't love the persona they'd created. "Why do I need to have a criminal record for passing bad checks?"

"If you're too squeaky clean, the scumbags won't be able to relate to you."

He returned to his minivan and dragged out a beat-up, filthy tarp. He didn't ask for her help, but stretching the tarp over the boxes would be easier with two people.

She picked up one end. "This thing looks like it went through a cattle stampede."

"Brady Gilliam wouldn't have a new tarp."

"Oh, good. Now you're referring to yourself in the third person."

"I'm not Gilliam yet."

She helped him spread the tarp and tie it down. "Where did Brady Gilliam get all this stuff?"

"I had some of it shipped from my home in Arlington, and I found the rest in army surplus and secondhand stores."

"You're kind of a compulsive planner, aren't you?"

He said nothing, which was fine with her. The question had been rhetorical. His compulsiveness was a given.

That tendency made him extremely vulnerable to teasing. She hadn't forgotten how he'd embarrassed her with his off-handed, unexpected marriage proposal, and she intended to get even.

He finished with the tarp and stepped back to admire his handiwork. "Thanks for volunteering the use of your truck."

"Sure thing." He'd already changed her Colorado license plates to California. "I don't even mind that you think my sweet, red, Toyota pickup is beat-up enough to belong to the itinerant Gilliam couple. I mean, sure, she's got a little rust and a couple of dents, but she looks good for a twelve-year-old truck."

"She's also got an oil leak and needs a tune-up."

He patted the side of the truck. "I could fix that for you."

"You?"

"My grandpa owns a car repair shop. I've worked for him since I was teenager."

A surprising bit of info. "You don't seem like the type who'd get his hands dirty."

"I wear gloves."

"Of course you do."

He wiped his forehead with the back of his hand. With his stubble and his sweat and his background as a car mechanic, he almost didn't seem like a fed…almost. He gave a nod. "I think we're ready to go."

"Really?" *Not until I get my revenge.* "Is that what you're going to wear?"

He looked down at his black T-shirt and cargo pants. "What's wrong with this?"

"Nothing, if you're Brady Masters, FBI agent. In that identity, it makes sense for you to wear a fitted black T-shirt and khaki cargo pants that still look new."

"They are new. Bought them yesterday."

"If you're going to pass yourself off as Brady Gilliam, we're going to have to grunge you up."

He faced her directly, and she had a momentary flashback to her sexy dreams. Whether he was a fed or an artist or anything else, Brady was a fine-looking man—tall and lean with wide shoulders.

Although his gray eyes were hidden behind sunglasses, the lower half of his face was expressive. When amused, his dimple appeared. Most of the time, his jaw was tight and determined—like it was right now.

"What makes you an expert on grunge?" he asked.

"Dude, I grew up in San Francisco and I went to college at Berkeley. I know what starving artists look like."

"Fine," he muttered. "I'm open to suggestions."

"Untuck your shirt and take off your socks."

Reluctantly, he did as she said. He cringed as he stuck his bare feet into his running shoes. "Happy?"

"Those sneakers look like they just walked out of a mall. Maybe you should wear sandals."

"I don't like sandals."

"You need to loosen up. Let your toes come out and breathe." She thoroughly enjoyed giving him a hard time. "And you've got to lose the wristwatch."

His right hand coiled protectively around his gold watchband. "Not the watch."

"Artists don't pay attention to time. Gilliam isn't the kind of guy who punches a time clock or makes appointments."

"It's a long drive. I'll take off the watch when we're close to Durango."

Her next bit of supposedly well-meaning advice was sure to push him over the edge. "You know what would make you really look like an out-of-work artist?"

"What?"

"A tattoo. Maybe a dragon starting on your wrist, going all the way up your arm and wrapping around your throat."

He recoiled as though she'd splashed him in the face with a bucket of ice water. "No tats. No way."

She smiled sweetly. Payback was fun. "I'm teasing."

"That was a joke?"

"I just wanted to get under your skin, no pun intended."

He exhaled through flared nostrils as he rubbed his un-tattooed forearm. "This undercover stuff doesn't come easy for me. I have to work at it."

"Because you're not a good liar?"

"Lying doesn't bother me. I have a hard time acting like somebody else. It's not natural. Cole suggested that I set up Brady Gilliam to reflect as much of my core personality as possible." He stuck his hand into his pocket. "Speaking of Gilliam, I should give you this ring."

She took the wedding band from him. To her surprise, it wasn't a cheap dime store ring. The band was white gold with a Celtic knot design. "Brady, this is beautiful."

"Even if I was a struggling artist and all-around failure, I'd want my beloved wife to have something special. That's the only kind of marriage I can imagine."

Just when she was beginning to think that she had the upper hand, he had disarmed her. She slipped the ring onto her finger. "A perfect fit."

"I'm glad you like it."

This occasion seemed to call for something more. A hug? A peck on the cheek? That might give him the wrong idea. They were only pretending to be married. She wasn't attracted to him. Okay, maybe she was a little bit attracted…

The uncomfortable moment ended when his cell phone rang and he answered. As he talked, he went to the passenger side of the truck and opened the door. They'd already decided that she'd take the first shift driving because she knew her way around the area. She climbed behind the steering wheel, fastened her seat belt and plugged her key into the ignition.

He ended his call and turned toward her. "That was Cole."

She started the engine. "Why did he call?"

"He's been coordinating with local law enforcement. During the past five months, three young women have gone missing from Denver."

"That's terrible, but it doesn't sound like a lot."

"All three were eight months pregnant."

A shudder wrenched through her. With the teasing and the packing and the rushing around, she'd almost forgotten why they were going undercover. This investigation wasn't a game. These missing women were victims of the worst kind of crime.

She worked with new mothers every day. There was no worse pain than losing a child.

Chapter Five

Her twelve-year-old truck didn't have GPS, but Brady trusted Petra to find the best route from Granby to Durango in the southwest corner of Colorado. If they got lost, he'd use the map function on his phone to get them back on track.

He took advantage of Petra's time behind the wheel to make some phone calls. Even though he'd be reporting his progress to the agent in charge of the ITEP task force, Brady had opted to use Cole McClure as his point man. Not only did Cole have years of undercover experience, but he also had a decent relationship with Colorado law enforcement. His information regarding the three missing pregnant women might prove useful.

By the time Brady got off the phone, they were well on their way, cruising on a paved, two-lane highway with wide shoulders. Petra drove five to ten miles over the speed limit, but he wasn't complaining. The weather was good, and the traffic was light. He settled back for a long drive—over three hundred miles crossing the Continental Divide and descending approximately a thousand feet in elevation. Near Durango, the average temperature would be nine to twelve degrees warmer, and the aspen leaves were just beginning to turn gold.

He leaned back against his seat. "I like a good road trip."

"Where are you from?" she asked.

"Texas."

"I thought I heard a bit of a drawl in your voice. Where in Texas?"

"Austin." He hesitated before saying more. "Cole told me that we should integrate as much of our real life as possible into our undercover identity. It's easier to remember."

"Is Brady Gilliam from Austin?"

He nodded. "Like me, he has a younger brother and a twin sister. My real twin, Barbara, is in the FBI, based in Manhattan. I think I'll have my undercover twin also live in New York City, but I'll say she's a schoolteacher."

Her window was down, and the breeze whipped through her long auburn hair. She used a paisley scarf as a headband, and the long ends draped over her shoulder. In her circle-shaped sunglasses, white muslin blouse and loose-fitting patterned trousers, she looked like a free spirit—not the type of woman he spent time with, much less married.

"When I was growing up," she said, "I wanted a twin. Somebody who was always on my side."

"Yeah, that's how it works in the movies."

"You sound bitter."

"Not anymore."

He'd made his peace with his miserable childhood. Staring through the windshield, he watched the rise and fall of rolling hills of dry, khaki-colored grasses. No longer did he waste time hating his alcoholic, abusive father—a man who came in and out of his life when the mood suited him. Long ago, Brady had given up trying to understand why his mother stayed loyal to the man she'd married at the expense of her children.

He still had the scars from the last time his father had given him a whipping. He'd just turned twelve and was almost as tall as his dad but half his size. After the old man beat him, he'd gone after Barbara. That had been when Brady fought back. His rage had given him the strength of a grown man. Every time he was knocked down, he'd gotten back up and fought even harder. His father left with a broken nose and never came back.

This horror story wasn't something he'd share with Petra. It was better to let her think that he and Barbara were the idyllic image of twins in matching colors.

He cleared his throat. "We've got a long drive ahead of us."

"Probably six hours."

"There are two things we need to accomplish." He brushed away the past and concentrated on a positive, rational agenda. "Number one, I should brief you on what to expect at the Lost Lamb Ranch. Number two, we'll firm up our undercover identities."

"Let's start with what Cole told you," she said. "You just got off the phone with him, right?"

He nodded. "He's sending me mug shots for the missing women in an email. We should both memorize the pictures."

"What did the police find when they investigated?"

"No leads."

"That's hard to believe. The disappearance of a pregnant woman is usually a high-priority, high-profile case."

"Not for these women," Brady said. "They weren't beloved daughters or wives. They were homeless. Nobody organized a neighborhood search party to find them."

"But somebody noticed. Somebody reported them missing."

"Drug addict friends who, needless to say,

didn't do much to cooperate with the authorities. It's entirely possible that these women took off for a couple of days and then showed up and nobody bothered to tell the police. Or they moved to another city."

Darkly, she said, "Or they fell into the hands of traffickers who wanted them and their babies."

"They prey on the homeless, the helpless. Pregnant women are an easy target. They're already vulnerable and scared. If somebody offered them a place to stay until they deliver their babies—a place like Lost Lamb Ranch—they'd jump at it."

"Tell me about the Lost Lamb."

"It's run by Francine Kelso, a woman in her forties who has a record as a hooker and was suspected of being a madam. She doesn't hide her past. Instead, she points to it with pride and claims to have turned over a new leaf."

Petra nodded. "She's operating out of the same playbook that we're using."

"How so?"

"You just told me to use parts of my real past to establish my undercover identity." She toyed with the pink crystal that hung from a silver chain around her neck. "That's what Francine is doing, using her real past to disguise what she's doing in the present."

He appreciated how perceptive Petra was. Her

insights seemed to come from an intuitive sense. "You're good at reading people."

"In my line of work, it helps to understand where somebody is coming from."

"How so?"

"When a woman goes into labor, all her defenses are down. The same goes for the husband. While some people respond to a firm tone of voice and detailed instructions, others need gentle coaxing. Everybody's different. One time, I delivered a baby for a couple who started in a pastel room doing deep breathing and playing soft classical music. By the time the mother was ready to push, they'd changed the tape to 'Welcome to Hell.' Both of them cursed like gangsters."

"What did you do?"

"I sang along." She laughed. "It was one of those times when I was glad to be doing a home birth. We were so loud that we would have freaked out the entire wing of a hospital. After the baby was born, the mom and dad went back to mellow."

The behavior sounded psychotic to him. "Did those parents often exhibit excessive rage?"

"Who talks like that? Exhibit excessive rage?" She took off her sunglasses so he could see her roll her eyes. "Never try to psychoanalyze a woman in labor. It's way too primal. And, by the way, these two are kind, loving, wonderful parents."

Brady was glad they had a long drive ahead of them. It was going to take him a while to get a handle on his partner. "Let's get back to Francine Kelso. Assuming the Lost Lamb Ranch is a kind of holding pen for these pregnant women, Francine is the warden. She keeps tabs on what's going on."

"How many people are at the ranch?"

"Francine's assistant is Margaret Woods, twenty-three years old, the mother of a three-year-old boy named Wesley. She does most of the housekeeping and shopping. There are four or five men, supposedly ranch hands who take care of the livestock."

"Hold on," she said. "Is this a working ranch?"

"Not really. They have horses, goats and chickens. And there's a garden."

Her expression turned pensive. "Lost Lamb sounds like it could be a great place for a woman in her last months of pregnancy. Very organic and relaxed. It's exactly the kind of place where I'd like to work."

"If it wasn't a front for crime."

In his years with the FBI, he'd learned not to judge a situation by its appearance. There were drug bosses who lived in beautiful palaces. A cat burglar might be surrounded by artistic masterpieces. There were handsome, charming con men who stole every penny from a pension fund and bankrupted widows and children.

Brady relied on his rational judgment to see past the exterior to the rotten core. His tendency was to expect the worst in others. That way he was never disappointed.

"How many expectant mothers?" she asked.

"Right now, there are five. All of them have proper identification and have signed documents for the immediate adoption of the babies. The paperwork is handled by an attorney in Durango, Stan Mancuso. He's somebody we need to investigate."

"What about the local sheriff and cops?"

"There's no reason to believe they're corrupt, but we can't look to them for assistance. We're undercover," he said. "It's just you and me, baby."

AFTER A LONG DAY OF driving, Petra took her last shift in the passenger seat. While sucking the pulp out of an orange, she studied the Lost Lamb file on Brady's laptop. Aerial photos of the ranch showed a main house, two barracks that probably served as bunkhouses, a garage and a horse barn with a corral. The large garden plot was bordered by a narrow stream. The whole property butted up to a forested hillside.

She didn't see fences or blockades to prevent the expectant mothers from escaping. Nor was the property isolated; other houses were less than five miles away. Anyone who wanted to escape from the ranch probably could. It didn't seem like these women were being held against their will. Was it possible that the ranch was what it claimed to be? A sanctuary for pregnant women with nowhere else to go?

The lack of evidence was why they needed this elaborate undercover investigation. She remembered the blanket with the logo and the sheep design that had been wrapped around baby Miguel. If there was the slightest chance that Lost Lamb Ranch was involved in trafficking infants, it was worth checking out.

After studying the mug shots for the missing women again, she closed the computer down and tossed her orange rind in the trash bag Brady placed between the seats. Then she used one of the hand wipes from the package he'd put in the glove compartment.

She glanced over at him. "We're almost there. Time to lose the wristwatch, buddy."

He slipped it off. "This pains me."

"I'm sure it does." She stashed the watch in the glove compartment next to the hand sanitizer.

During the drive, they'd been stitching together the fabric of their undercover marriage and had decided that the Gilliams were happy with each other but financially down on their luck, which was why they jumped at the chance to move into a rent-free house in Durango.

The FBI techs had provided their undercover selves with fake former employers in case anybody bothered to check into their backgrounds. She was supposed to have worked as a midwife and with Berkeley Baby Clinic. When Brady Gilliam wasn't trying to sell his art, he had a part-time job as a car mechanic.

She wiggled her butt lower in her seat and elevated her legs, resting her heels on the dashboard. "We never figured out how Brady and Patty Gilliam met."

"I've got an idea," Brady said. "I saw you in a tavern, told you that you were beautiful and asked you to pose for me in the nude."

"Oh, please. Patty has street smarts. No way would she fall for a line like that."

"Maybe I invited you to my place to see my artwork."

She made gagging noises in the back of her throat. "Even worse."

"Okay, Ms. Street Smart, you tell me."

In the fading light of sunset, she studied his profile. After a day of driving with the wind coming through the windows, he'd lost all semblance of grooming. His thick hair was longer than she'd thought, especially in the back where it curled at his nape. His stubble outlined his chin. Some men could pull off the unkempt look without appearing grungy, and Brady was one of them. She was hit by a sudden urge to stroke her hand through his rough stubble and then to trace his lips. *Bad idea.*

"I'm waiting," he said. "How did the Gilliams meet?"

Keeping in mind the rule of sticking to reality, she tried to think of what she found attractive about him. The image that popped into her head was the moment when he launched himself through the air, risking everything to rescue Consuela.

"Here's the story," she said. "I was jogging on the Esplanade in San Francisco at dusk. It was foggy and mysterious and the air smelled like fish. Then, I heard a scream."

"Please don't tell me I'm a screamer."

"Not you. A woman had her purse stolen. And you took off in pursuit of the thief. Diving through the air, you tackled the bad guy and got the purse away from him."

"Okay." He nodded. "I'm liking this story."

She lifted her feet off the dashboard and sat up straight in her seat. "The thief had a knife and he cut your arm."

"Stop right there. I don't have a scar on my arm."

"Where do you have scars?"

"I blew out my knee playing football. We can say I landed on my knee and the old injury acted up."

"And that's where I come in," she said. "Because I'm a nurse, I patched you up."

"You can do that? I thought midwives just did baby stuff."

"I'm a certified nurse-midwife, and also an RN. I'd need that much training to work in California. They have strict licensing procedures."

He grinned. "The Gilliams met as crime fighters. Damn, I'm beginning to like this couple."

So was she. The idea of being married to him was growing on her. She'd been wondering about sleeping arrangements but figured Brady would have a solution. A man who planned far enough ahead to bring his own brand of bottled water would surely have worked out the details of who slept where.

For the last leg of the trip, he'd been using the GPS on his cell phone. About twelve miles from Durango, he exited the main road. A road sign indicated they were entering Kirkland. The town was so small that if you blinked, you missed it.

"I want to swing past the Lost Lamb before it gets dark," he said.

"Fine by me."

After they'd driven some distance, he consulted the map on his phone. "At the fork in the road,

I go left to the Lost Lamb. Our house is to the right."

She noticed that he'd said "our house" instead of "the Gilliams' house." Their relationship was changing. "Should we start being Patty and Brady Gilliam now?"

"From now until the investigation is over."

"It's the first time I've been married."

"Me, too."

With her thumb, she rubbed the Celtic knot pattern on her wedding band. "I don't feel any different."

"When you're married for real," he said, "you will."

He spoke with the absolute confidence that she found annoying. "How do you know for sure?"

"Logic," he said.

"Just because you're certain, it doesn't mean you're right."

Daylight was almost gone, and he should have turned on his headlights. She assumed he was trying to be subtle as they neared the ranch. Rounding a curve, she spotted two women walking on the gravel shoulder of the road. "Watch out."

"I see them."

She noticed that one of the women was pregnant. If she was from Lost Lamb, this was an opportunity for Petra to introduce herself. "Pull over."

"Why?"

"Pull over. Now."

He braked, and the red truck came to a sudden stop. Petra hopped out and ran back toward the two women.

"Are you all right?" she asked. "I hope we didn't scare you."

"We're fine."

Petra recognized the not-pregnant woman from a photo in the computer file. This was Margaret Woods, the twenty-three-year-old housekeeper at Lost Lamb. In her jeans and pink hoodie sweatshirt, she looked younger. Nervously, she chewed her lower lip and pushed her straight brown hair out of her eyes.

With a friendly smile, Petra stuck out her hand. "We're new in town. I'm Patty Gilliam."

Shaking hands, Margaret introduced herself and a pregnant woman with a belly the size of a blimp. Her girth was covered by a truly awful flowered muumuu. "Her name is Deandra but we call her Dee."

"Well, Dee," Petra said, "I'm guessing you're past your due date. That's why you're out for a walk. You're hoping the physical activity will get your labor started."

"Yeah, walking." Dee scoffed. Below a curly

fringe of blond hair, her face pinched in an angry knot. "Sounds like an old wives' tale to me."

"The thing about old wives is that they know a lot about practical solutions." Petra liked to try all the noninvasive, natural remedies before resorting to induced labor. "Walking is a good idea because when your hips swing back and forth, it gets things moving. Eating spicy food might also bring on labor. Or having sex."

Suspiciously, Margaret asked, "How do you know so much about labor?"

"I'm a midwife," Petra announced. "And I'm glad you asked because I'm setting up a practice right here in this area. So if you know any other pregnant wom—"

"We have to be going," Margaret interrupted.

Brady strode toward them. "Ladies, I'm so sorry if my driving startled you."

Petra introduced him as her husband—a fact that was largely ignored by both of these young women who responded immediately to his very masculine presence. Brady was fresh meat, and these ladies were starving.

"So glad," Margaret said breathily, "to meet you."

"I should have turned my headlights on," Brady said. "But I was admiring the shadows and the fading light on the tree branches. I'm an artist."

His two admirers nearly swooned.

He asked, "Can we give you a lift?"

Margaret retreated to her cautious attitude. "No, thanks. We're almost home."

Dee gave a little gasp and looked down. The gravel beneath her sneakers was wet.

"Congratulations," Petra said. "Your water broke."

Chapter Six

Never in his life had Brady felt so helpless. He would have preferred facing a dozen Mafia hitmen to being stranded on a country road with a pregnant woman about to go into labor. His natural inclination was to hide behind his badge of authority—to whip out his cell phone, call for an ambulance and start giving orders. But that behavior didn't suit his undercover identity as a laid-back artist.

He shot a panicked glance toward Petra. Why the hell had she jumped out of the truck with no plan in mind?

"Not to worry," Petra said as she wrapped her arm around Dee's shoulder. "Sometimes it takes a day or even longer after the water breaks for labor to start. Have you been having contractions?"

"I don't know. What's it supposed to feel like?"

"Everybody's different. A contraction might be a sharp pain or just a cramp."

"Cramps. Yes." Dee's voice went shrill. "I have cramps. Oh, my God, the baby's coming."

"Calm down," Margaret snapped. "You'd think you were the first woman to ever give birth."

"Here's what we're going to do," Petra said as she pointed Dee toward the truck. "The first thing is to take you home so you can change clothes and get comfortable. Come along with me. I'll drive you there."

Legs apart, Dee waddled along beside her. "I want drugs. None of this natural childbirth crud. Lots of drugs."

Margaret bounded around them like a yappy little terrier. "Leave us alone. She'll be fine. I can take care of her."

"I'm sure you can," Petra said calmly, "but Dee's comfort is the most important thing. How far are we from where you live?"

"Half a mile."

"The truck has only two seats, so I'll drive there with Dee. You and Brady can walk. Right, Brady?"

This was his cue to speak, and he managed to gurgle out an affirmative response. This impromptu turn of events was actually to their advantage; taking Dee home gave them a believable reason to gain entrance to Lost Lamb. But they were so damn disorganized.

He fell into step with Margaret who was walking as fast as her short, little legs could carry her. "I'm in so much trouble," she said. "Miss Francine doesn't like for us to get involved with the locals."

"Relax," he advised, though his heart was racing. "This is an emergency."

"Not really. Dee is a big fat cow who is going to be in labor for hours after this, and she'll be whining and sobbing. Some women just aren't good at having babies."

"My wife could help her." It was strangely comforting to refer to Petra as his wife. "She's good at what she does."

Down the road, he saw the taillights of the truck turn right. Beside him, Margaret groaned. "So much trouble."

As an FBI agent, he wouldn't be friendly or approachable, but Brady Gilliam was more casual. He patted Margaret's shoulder. "I'm sure you'll be just fine."

Her frightened brown eyes searched his face. "Really?"

"You seem like a real sweet girl who was just helping her pregnant friend. Who could be mad about that?"

Tears spilled down her cheeks. "You have no idea."

"Tell me," he urged. "Margaret, you can tell me anything."

Instead of confiding, she picked up her heels

and took off like a jackrabbit, dashing toward the open gate where the truck had turned. He hoped he hadn't spooked her. The nervous, little housekeeper could be a good source of information about the operation at Lost Lamb.

PETRA PARKED THE TRUCK close to the veranda that stretched across the front of the main house. The aerial photos of the Lost Lamb compound had been accurate, showing the two-story, white house with a horse barn to the left and outbuildings at the rear. But the view from above didn't capture the atmosphere.

This should have been a homey place—a ranch house where the family would gather in rocking chairs and talk about their day. Instead, there was an impersonal, institutional air as though no one lived here long enough to put down roots. A metal sign—Lost Lamb Ranch—hung from the railing on the covered veranda that stretched all the way across the front of the house. Another sign posted by the door advised No Smoking.

The veranda was tidy, recently swept. Three steps led to the door. Beside them was a long, plywood wheelchair ramp. Dim lights shone through the windows on the first floor, but the upstairs was dark and foreboding.

A pregnant woman in jeans and a tight yellow T-shirt rose from a rocking chair and stood at the railing watching. The corners of her mouth pulled down in an exaggerated scowl. "What's going on?"

"Hi, there." Petra waved. Then she opened the passenger door for Dee and helped her out of the truck. "I found this lady on the road. Her water broke."

"About time." The pregnant woman went to the front door, opened it and yelled. "Miss Francine, it's Dee. She's in labor."

As soon as Dee got out, she flung her arm around Petra's neck and hung on her like a pregnant sandbag. She gave a loud, exaggerated moan. "I'm in pain. I need drugs."

Petra was grateful that the women she usually worked with were positive, upbeat and motivated to have natural childbirth. Someone like Dee needed to be handled like a diva with lavish attention and gobs of compliments.

Looking into Dee's squinty eyes, Petra smiled warmly. "You're so brave."

"I am?"

"Oh, yes, you have inner strength. I can see it. You're glowing with it."

"I'm glowing?"

"There's nothing more beautiful in the world than a pregnant woman."

"Me? Beautiful?"

The front door opened and Francine Kelso appeared. She was a dramatic presence. Her shining, shoulder-length black curls were too perfectly coiffed to be anything but a wig, and her elaborate black eyeliner evoked images of Cleopatra. She wore black leggings and jeweled sandals. Even though she was slim, her cleavage spilled over the bedazzled edge of her low-cut, turquoise top. Her dossier said she was a former hooker/madam. It didn't take much imagination to see her as a dominatrix.

From the veranda, she glared down at Petra. "Who the hell are you?"

"Patty Gilliam. My husband and I just moved to the area. We almost ran into Dee and Margaret on the road, so we stopped to see if they were all right. It's lucky we came along. Dee's water broke."

"I'm in labor," Dee wailed. "I need a doctor."

This was the opening Petra had been hoping for. "I'm not sure if it's time to call the OB-GYN, but I'd be happy to stay and help out until you decide what to do. I'm a certified nurse-midwife."

"That's handy," Francine said coolly.

Petra nodded toward the sign that hung from the railing. "Lost Lamb Ranch? Because you have two very pregnant ladies here, I'm guessing you're not sheep herders."

"This is a home for unwed mothers."

Instead of inviting them in or rushing to take

care of Dee, Francine blocked their way like a sentry, which made Petra aware of the secrets she was guarding.

Dee sagged against her, and Petra had to exert an effort to stay standing. She took a step forward. This was her excuse to get inside the house and have a look around. "We need to get Dee out of these wet clothes."

From behind her back, she heard Margaret cry out. "I've got her. I'll take it from here."

"I'm weak," Dee moaned. "I'm going to faint."

Margaret, who was out of breath from running, grabbed Dee's other arm just in time. Even with both of them holding her, the pregnant woman was slipping from their grasp as she fainted.

In a bit of perfect timing, Brady came to the rescue. He caught Dee under her knees and around her shoulders. With an effort, he lifted her.

"My husband, Brady," Petra said to Francine. "I don't believe I caught your name."

"Francine Kelso. I'm in charge here."

"Great," Brady said. "Where should I put this lady?"

"Drop her on the porch," Margaret snapped. "She's faking."

Even though Petra agreed that Dee's swoon probably wasn't the real thing, she was determined to get inside. She climbed the stairs and confronted Francine directly. "I'm sure you have the proper facilities. Brady should carry Dee to your clinic or birthing room where she can be examined."

Francine's gaze held a full measure of hostility, but there was also calculation in her heavily made-up eyes. Lost Lamb had a reputation to protect. She couldn't have Petra and Brady telling people that she wasn't treating these young women well.

"Follow me." She pivoted and entered the house.

Petra held the door for Brady who carried his heavy burden without too much effort. As he trailed Francine down a carpeted hallway, he glanced to the right and nodded to another pregnant woman who sprawled across a sofa in a living room area, furnished with unremarkable sofas and chairs in various shades of beige and brown.

To the left of the front foyer and staircase, Petra glimpsed an office with a gorgeous Aubusson rug, an antique cherry desk and a credenza with fresh flowers. She guessed that the left was Francine's side of the house, and it was furnished with far more care and expense than the area used by the other denizens of this institution. The hallway led past a dining area with a long table and into an institutional kitchen where two Hispanic women— one pregnant and the other not—were washing dishes.

With each woman she encountered, Petra studied their features, comparing them to the mug shots from the Missing Persons files. None matched. All these women were young. Some appeared to be nervous, and others were hostile.

"Move along," Margaret said brusquely. "And don't stare."

"I'm not," Petra said.

"You're judging them. Everybody who comes here does. They think bad things about these girls because they got pregnant."

Petra stopped short at the edge of the kitchen. She should have kept going, trying to get on the good side of Francine, but she couldn't let this accusation go unanswered. "I'd never look down on another woman because she was pregnant. Having a baby is the highest calling in life. Even after delivering dozens of babies, I'm still amazed. A pregnant woman is a miracle."

Margaret pulled her bangs off her forehead and stared. For an instant, the anger in her eyes softened. "You're telling the truth."

"I don't lie," Petra said. "It's bad karma."

"We shouldn't keep Francine waiting."

Beyond the kitchen was an examination room that was large, white and sterile. Stacked on one of the stainless steel countertops were several of the yellow blankets with the lamb design. Brady had placed Dee on the table with stirrups, and Francine was talking on a cell phone.

Instead of lying down, Dee had wakened enough to loudly complain. "I want a bath. And new clothes. I don't want to be here."

Gently, Petra brushed Brady out of the way and stood in front of Dee. She piled on the attention. "Are you all right? We were concerned when you fainted."

"You're right to worry." Dee pouted. "I'm very delicate."

"Like a cow," Margaret muttered under her breath.

With a glance toward Francine who was still on her cell phone, Petra decided to take action. If she asked for permission, she would surely be refused. Instead, she took the blood pressure cuff from the countertop and wrapped it around Dee's upper arm. "Let's make sure you're all right. The mother's well-being is vital to a successful birth."

"I just want this thing out of me."

That thing is a baby. Even though Petra was beginning to agree with the way Margaret felt about Dee, she held back her irritation and focused on the task at hand. Using a stethoscope, she took a blood pressure reading. "You're one-fifty-five over ninety. It's a little high."

Dee grasped her hand and squeezed hard. "I'm going to be okay, aren't I?"

"The elevated blood pressure could indicate hypertension." She removed the cuff. "But it's not high enough to worry about for you or for the baby."

"My baby boy is all right, isn't he?"

"You know you're having a son?"

"I've known for a long time. Is he okay?"

Her blue eyes opened wide, and Petra saw her fear. Dee wasn't really an obnoxious, unfeeling diva. She was scared and didn't seem to be getting much support from the other women in the house.

With utmost gentleness, Petra stroked the blond wisps off Dee's forehead. "You're both going to be fine. Giving birth is the most natural thing in the world. You can do this."

"It's going to hurt." Her voice caught on a sob. "I don't want it to hurt."

"You are going to feel some pain, but I know a great many techniques to deal with it. What's your favorite kind of music? Not for dancing but for when you're alone and relaxed."

"Show tunes. When I was in high school, I was one of the stars in *Oklahoma!*" A hint of a smile touched her mouth. "I had a solo number about the gal who couldn't say no. I guess it came true."

"I'll bet you were beautiful on stage." She pulled Brady into the conversation. "Don't you think so, honey?"

"Yeah, you must have been pretty."

It was clear that his attention was elsewhere. He'd positioned himself so his back was to the wall and he faced the doorway where Francine stood. Had he picked up on a threat that Petra had missed? Margaret seemed to have vanished. Did that mean anything?

"Oh, my, Brady." Dee fluttered her lashes. Apparently, she'd recovered enough to flirt. "Brady, you carried me in here. You're my hero."

"No problem," he said.

"And it will never happen again," Francine said coldly. She rested her back against the doorjamb, and folded her arms below her breasts. "You girls don't need to be rescued. You have to learn how to stand on your own two feet."

There was truth to what she was saying. Self-reliance counted as an important character trait, but Petra was willing to cut Dee some slack. *After* she had the baby, she could work on improving her character.

Francine turned her gaze on Petra. "You claim to be a midwife."

"I'm certified, licensed and ready to go," Petra said. "If you like, I can provide all kinds of references. I'd love to work here at Lost Lamb."

"You may leave your card."

Mission accomplished! She'd made contact and would be able to return. After this, the investigation would be easy. "We're so new in town that I don't have cards printed up yet. Brady, would you write down our address and phone number?"

"Sure." He smiled at Francine. "Have you got paper and pencil?"

Unlike Margaret and Dee, Francine wasn't impressed by his charms. She pulled open a drawer beside the sink and took out a pen and a yellow legal pad which she handed to him. "Why did you move here?"

"My aunt passed away a couple of years ago and left her cabin to me. It's been rented out, and that gave us some income. But the renters moved. Me and Patty decided to give Colorado a try." He scribbled down the address. "I'm going to be looking for work, too. If you hear anything—"

A big man in a flat brim hat filled the doorway. "We got no work here."

Petra hadn't heard him approach, which was surprising given his mountainous girth and the fact that he was wearing boots. She wondered how long he'd been eavesdropping.

Francine said, "This is Robert. He's one of our handymen and has clearly forgotten his manners. Your hat, sir."

"Yes, ma'am." He snatched it off his head. His greasy black hair hung nearly to his shoulders. His thick neck supported an overlarge head with heavy jowls. A paunch spilled over his belt, but he didn't look soft. With those huge shoulders, he could probably lift a buffalo. Plus, he was wearing a holster on his belt—not exactly standard equipment for a handyman.

Smiling, she introduced herself and Brady. Robert nodded an acknowledgment but didn't shake hands. Instead, he held out palms the size of baseball mitts and smeared with grease.

"You've been doing some car repair," Brady said. "I might be able to help out. I'm a mechanic."

"Actually," Petra said, "he's an artist."

"But working on cars and trucks pays the bills," Brady concluded.

"If we have need of your services," Francine said, "we'll be in touch."

"I appreciate it," Petra said.

"Robert will show you out the back door and accompany you to your truck."

"Don't go," Dee said plaintively. "Please, please, don't leave."

When Francine approached her, she went silent.

Even if Petra hadn't known that the Lost Lamb was involved in illegal activities, she would have thought the atmosphere was a weird mix—frightened pregnant women, nervous Margaret, Francine the dominatrix and Robert who was the size of an ogre.

Petra couldn't wait to come back here and investigate.

Chapter Seven

As Brady drove away from the Lost Lamb, he watched the giant figure of Robert recede in his rearview mirror. The guy was huge. Worse, he moved with the agility of an athlete. If Francine had ordered her so-called handyman to throw them off her property, the situation could have turned ugly. They'd been damn lucky to escape into the night without serious injury.

"That went well," Petra said.

He wasn't in the mood for joking. "Not funny."

"I wasn't going for a laugh." She had the nerve to sound insulted. "That was a good meet."

"It was disorganized. We should have had a plan, a goal, an agenda. In the future, I don't want you to jump in feet first with no idea of what you're going to encounter. That's how you get hurt."

Even as he spoke, he knew she wouldn't listen to his warning. Petra was as impulsive as a cat. She'd plunge wildly and then figure out how to land on her feet.

Her behavior didn't surprise him. Her psychological profile from Quantico labeled her as a risk-taker, similar to Cole McClure who had the reputation of being an incredible undercover agent. As irritating as he found her impulsiveness, her personality type was well suited to quick thinking and adaptability. He hoped her risky actions would work to their advantage without getting them killed.

"We accomplished a lot," she said. "We got inside Lost Lamb under a reasonable pretext. We saw four out of the five pregnant women who are supposed to be staying there. Plus, I got a chance to show my stuff, even if it was only taking blood pressure. If you ask me, we did good, really good."

"You were believable," he conceded.

"How could I not be? I'm playing the role of a midwife. And guess what? That's what I do, all the time, every day. Easy-peasy."

"For me? Not so much." His undercover identity as a laid-back artist fit him like a glove on a foot. He knew enough about art to pull off the occupational part of that equation, but there was nothing easygoing about him.

"Francine believes I'm a pro," Petra said. "She asked for my card."

"Because she intends to check us out," he said. "She's probably on the phone right now, talking to that lawyer in Durango to make sure we're who we say we are."

"We've got nothing to worry about," she countered. "Your FBI techies have our undercover identities in place. When Francine is satisfied that we're cool, she'll invite me to come back and deliver babies."

"You can't go back there alone."

"Why not?"

Dozens of reasons exploded inside his head like buckshot pellets. Her lack of training. The unpredictability of the situation. The desperate nature of human trafficking. Mostly, he'd never forgive himself if he sent her off by herself and something happened to her.

"It's too dangerous," he said. "You saw Robert. The guy is bigger than a double-wide refrigerator."

"And armed, too. But Francine has him on a tight leash." She leaned forward in the passenger seat to look at him. "Was it just me or did she have a Mistress of the Dark vibe?"

He wouldn't be surprised to find thigh-high leather boots and whips in her closet. "She sure as hell doesn't look like the matron of a home for unwed mothers."

"I wonder who delivers the babies. Somehow, I don't see Francine ruining her manicure with a messy delivery."

"What about Margaret?"

"Sweet, little Margaret." Petra chuckled. "She's got a crush on you."

"Maybe," he said.

"There's nothing maybe about it. When she shook your hand, she was practically drooling."

He braked, and the truck's headlights shone on a stop sign that was pocked with bullet holes. They were back at the fork in the road where the left turn led to Lost Lamb and the right would take them to their cabin.

A lot had happened in the past forty-five minutes. He looked over at Petra. Even though she had her seat belt on, she was sitting with her legs tucked up in a yoga position. She radiated calm. No fussing. No fidgeting.

Her smile was a challenge. The spark in her eyes invited him to engage with him. "You know I'm right," she said.

For a moment, he had the idea that her teasing was sexual, that she wanted him to come closer. "Right about what?"

"Margaret has the hots for you."

He didn't care about Margaret or any other woman. Petra filled his vision. He watched the rise and fall of the white muslin fabric that draped softly over her breasts. Her thick, auburn hair framed her face.

Leaning a few inches closer, he realized how much he wanted to kiss her, to brush his fingers through her tangled hair, to inhale the scent of wildflowers that seemed to surround her. All day long, his attraction had been growing. His inappropriate attraction.

He reined in his desire. What had they been talking about? Something about Margaret having a crush on him? He raised an eyebrow. "Jealous?"

"Of you and Margaret? Hah!"

Facing the windshield, he drove past the stop sign. "Think of yourself as Patty Gilliam, my wife. Do we have that kind of relationship? Are you the jealous type?"

"Because we're basing our undercover selves on our real selves, I'd have to say that I'm really attached to the people I love. I couldn't care less about things, though. Like Gandhi says, the earth provides enough for our need, not our greed."

"How did we go from jealousy to Gandhi?"

"What about you?" she asked. "Are you possessive?"

"In the sense that I appreciate my possessions and take good care of them, I'd have to say yes."

"Like your superlight bulletproof vest?"

"And my gun."

"That's not very undercover of you."

"Can't help it."

If she didn't quit teasing, he'd have to retaliate.

He knew exactly how to get the upper hand with someone who liked to take risks. All he had to do was toss out a dare, and she'd respond.

"We still haven't figured out if Margaret is acting as a midwife," she said. "Maybe you should do a profiler analysis on her."

Maybe he should. It would be a relief to slip into professional mode. He knew how to size up suspects and witnesses from a brief encounter. That was his training, and he was seventy-percent accurate in his initial assessments.

"She's running on fear. Francine scares her, but Margaret still respects her and calls her Miss Francine, indicating a desperate need for approval." He recalled from Margaret's profile that she had a three-year-old son. "She's such a waif-like creature that it's hard to imagine her being a mother. But I'd guess that she loves her child with all her heart, partly because she knows her toddler son won't abandon her."

"And everybody else has," Petra said. "I got that feeling from her, too. She's so alone in the world that her loyalties are all messed up. She can work for these bad people and rationalize that it's okay."

"But she knows what's going on. Her understanding of right and wrong is one reason why she's scared," he said. "Margaret might be a good source of information for us."

"Do you think she delivers the babies?"

"She could assist, but the responsibility of a medical procedure would be too much for her to handle. I doubt she can do the kind of work you do."

"That means there are other people at the Lost Lamb," Petra said. "We need to get inside and really take a look around. I could go back tomorrow under the pretext of checking on Dee."

"We'll make a plan," he said firmly.

Even though there were no street lights on this curving rural road, the moonlight showed an open field behind a barbed wire fence. On the other side were occasional houses with lights from the windows. After a long day of driving, he couldn't wait to get out of the truck and decompress. Soon, they'd be home.

"Tell me about the house," Petra said. "How big is it?"

"Three bedrooms, one bath. It's owned by the government and occasionally used as a safe house. The last residents were a couple in witness protection. From what I understand, it's furnished."

"And yet, you brought a truckload of stuff."

"It's my cover," he said. "I'm going to turn one of the bedrooms into an art studio."

"And the other bedrooms?"

"One for you and one for me."

He was attracted to her. That was for damn sure. During their six-hour drive, he'd been captivated watching her gesture with hands as graceful as butterflies. Her hair enticed him. She was always stretching and changing position, amazingly limber. More than once, he'd imagined her long legs wrapped around him.

But he wouldn't touch her. It was against the rules. Unprofessional. He wouldn't make a mistake that could compromise their mission and derail his career.

Sleeping with Petra wasn't part of the plan.

IT HAD BEEN YEARS SINCE Petra lived with a man, and now she was moving in with Brady—a guy she barely knew but had fantasized about. Living together was going to be difficult on many levels.

For one thing, she couldn't do whatever she wanted, whenever she wanted. Not that she had a lot of rude habits. But she was a night owl who sometimes played music and exercised at two in the morning.

And she wasn't the tidiest person in the world. Her clutter would drive Brady up the wall, which was just too bad for him. He was the one who proposed after all. For better or worse?

She grinned to herself. They weren't married.

She definitely wasn't going to start thinking of him *that* way. He wasn't her spouse or even her boyfriend. At best, they were partners.

He pulled up in front of the two-story cedar house. "We're home."

A balcony with a railing separated the top and bottom of the house. A couple of hummingbird feeders dangled from hooks attached to the lower side of the balcony. The two windows on either side of the front door had the shades drawn as though the house was asleep. "I like this place."

"It's not bad." Brady maneuvered the truck until the back bumper was closest to the door. "The sight lines are clear in three directions. The only way somebody can sneak up on us is through the forest at the rear."

Of course, he'd be concerned about security. "Is there an alarm system?"

"We're on our own."

Those words triggered a response in her—a surge of excitement. This was something new for her, something different, an adventure.

They got out of the truck and crossed the flagstones leading to the entrance. Brady unlocked the front door, pushed it open, reached inside and turned on the porch light. Standing under the glow, he flashed a grin. "Should I carry you over the threshold, Mrs. Gilliam?"

She hesitated before answering. She wasn't overly superstitious, but she appreciated the wisdom in old wives' tales. Like most traditions, there was a basis for the groom lifting the bride into her new home. If she stumbled on her way inside, it brought bad luck upon the house. But Petra wasn't really a bride, so it shouldn't count. "Not necessary."

Carefully stepping over the door, she followed him inside. The front room had a moss rock fireplace and a couple of earth-tone sofas. Two of the walls were paneled with knotty pine. A long counter, also knotty pine, separated the front room from a kitchen with a terra-cotta floor. The whole effect was unspectacular but pleasant. The warm glow of the wood felt welcoming. "Who did you say lived here before?"

"A husband and wife in the witness protection program. I don't know anything more than that."

To the left of the front door was a rugged wood staircase. As she climbed, she said, "It seems like witness protection would be a huge trauma. First, there's a horrible crime. Then they're torn away from their families and friends. These people might have left behind some bad juju."

"Some what?"

"Negative energy."

The upstairs consisted of a landing, three bedrooms and a bathroom. After she'd turned on all the lights, she claimed the bedroom that overlooked the front entrance. "This one is mine. I like the blue walls."

He stood in the doorway watching her. With his stubble and disheveled hair, he looked as rugged and sexy as the man who invaded her dreams last night. "Blue is your color. It goes with your eyes."

"That's sort of an artistic observation, Mr. Gilliam."

"I like art. It's rational, all about proportion."

She needed to keep that in mind because her response to him seemed to be growing out of proportion. The cute little house wrapped around them with a warm intimacy. The surrounding forest felt too silent. She was intensely aware of being alone with him.

"I should get unpacked," she said.

It took less than an hour for her to unload her boxes, unpack her clothes and make the bed, using some of the bed linens Brady had brought with them. His sheets were ice blue, a million thread count and smooth as a caress. The man might be compulsive, but he had excellent taste.

On the dresser, she set out some of her personal belongings: a framed family photo, a beaded jewelry box, a purple crystal dolphin and a green earthenware bowl with a lotus design. She stepped back and took a look at the blank walls and hardwood floor with a blue-and-gray rag rug next to the bed.

This place didn't feel like home. She wasn't going to live here for long, so no need to put down roots. But she needed to be comfortable enough to think clearly.

From the suitcase she'd stashed in the closet, she took out a wooden box carved with an intricate design. Inside were three six-inch-long packets of dried sage, shaped like cigars and tied with sweet grass twine. When she opened the lid, a musky scent unfurled through her bedroom.

She'd gathered and dried these herbs herself. Then she'd braided the sweet grass into twine and wrapped the sage. The end result was a smudge stick, used to cleanse negative energy from the environment.

The origin of the smudging ceremony was either Celtic or Wiccan or Native American. Petra didn't know for sure. When she was fifteen, she and her sister developed their own procedure, lighting the sage and wafting the smoke in the doorways and corners of a room to absorb the bad juju. She liked the idea of using smoke—something she feared—to a good purpose.

She wasn't sure if smudging had any effect. Probably not, but the process made her feel better. On those occasions when she'd smudged a labor room, the pregnant women usually said the smoke relaxed them. In any case, her smudging ceremony couldn't hurt.

The problem would be to convince Brady.

Chapter Eight

Petra skipped down the staircase to the front room where several boxes were neatly stacked by the fireplace. Brady was behind the counter in the kitchen, unloading dinnerware. He moved as quickly and efficiently as a robot, but he was definitely all man. The sinews in his forearms flexed and extended with striking precision. A sheen of sweat glistened on his forehead. He could have been doing reps in a gym instead of lifting plates and bowls.

He glanced toward her. "All settled?"

"Mostly."

She was absolutely certain that he wouldn't like her smudging ceremony. Super-rational Brady wasn't the type of person who believed in magic, and she didn't expect him to change. But she needed for him to withhold his disdain. If he started scoffing, the negative energy would multiply instead of vanish.

"Did you come to help?" he asked.

"Yes." Smudging counted as being helpful.

"Good. We'll run these dishes through the washer before putting them away on the shelves."

From what she could see, he'd brought along enough tableware and cookware to open a restaurant. The top of the counter was littered with pots and pans, which she pushed aside to make room. She placed the smudge stick and her green lotus bowl on the countertop, then she jumped up and sat beside them with her legs dangling. "Why did you bring so much stuff?"

"Makes sense for our undercover identity," he said. "If anybody comes snooping around, they'll see a fully equipped kitchen. Plus, we need something to cook with. The nearest restaurant is miles away, and I doubt they deliver."

"Didn't we pass a little town on the way here?"

"Kirkland," he said. "Population eighty-two including the jackrabbits."

"Every small town has a diner where the locals gather. A good place to get information about Lost Lamb."

"That's smart." He crossed the terra-cotta-tiled kitchen floor to stand in front of her. "We should make a point of hanging out at the diner."

"Especially you." She pointed at the center of his chest. "You need to make friends because you're looking for work."

He smiled just enough to activate his dimple.

The rest of his features—forehead, jaw, cheek-bones and brow—were chiseled and rugged. The dimple gave her hope that he might have a bit of sensitivity.

His nostrils twitched, and he looked down at the countertop. "What's in that bowl? It smells weird."

Hoping to introduce him gradually to her plan, she picked up the lotus bowl. "This was made by a friend of mine from San Francisco. Sometimes, I use it to burn incense. Mostly, I like the design. The bowl reminds me of her."

"And the stinky stuff?"

"It's a smudge stick, made of sage and sweet grass. I use it for a ritual."

"Uh-huh." His gaze turned guarded and skeptical.

"Don't worry," she said. "I don't expect you to start chanting. Just be neutral. Don't put out grumpy vibes."

"What kind of ritual? Is this a witchy thing?" He rested the flat of his hand on the countertop and leaned closer, invading her personal space. "Are you going to get naked?"

"Why would you think that?"

"Isn't that what witches do? Take off their clothes and dance around a bonfire in the moon-light?"

His attitude irritated her. "This is exactly what

I expected from you. And exactly what I don't need. Will you please just be quiet?"

"Hey, I can keep an open mind. Tell me what you want."

"I need matches."

From one of the drawers, he took out a box of wooden matches which he handed to her. He stepped back and watched as she lit the sage, allowed it to burn for a moment and blew it out. Fragrant smoke drifted toward the ceiling.

Holding the smudge stick in her right hand, she recited a blessing that she and her sister had made up for their ritual. "May this house be filled with light and affirmation. As the smoke rises, may it absorb negativity. In this home, we will be safe and happy."

The first part of the process was to wipe away the bad thoughts she carried with her. Lowering the smudge stick to her bare feet, she slowly raised it from the floor to the chakra at the top of her head. The smoke drew the negative emotions—anger, fear and hate—to the surface.

She acknowledged those feelings. They were as much a part of her as generosity, nurturing and love. It would take more than a smudge stick to banish the dark side of her personality. For now, she'd concentrate on the light. She exhaled in a whoosh, blowing those feelings away.

"There," she said, "I'm cleansed."

"Do me." He waited, arms hanging loosely at his side.

She regarded him with a healthy dose of suspicion. Did he really have an open mind or was he teasing again? "Close your eyes and breathe deeply."

He did as she said, and she repeated the process with him. The sage burned more brightly as she outlined his body. "Your aura is strong."

"If you say so."

"I do."

She didn't pretend that her ritual was sacred. Her process didn't precisely follow any pattern that she was aware of. But smudging made her feel better, and she didn't want him laughing at her.

When he opened his eyes, she saw nothing but acceptance. Gently, he said, "I won't pretend that I understand what you're doing, but I'm all in favor of positive energy."

"Okay." She was still hesitant. They'd been teasing each other all day.

"You can trust me," he said.

That was a big promise, and a very big step for her. She wanted to believe him. "Come with me while I do the rest of the house."

She waved the stick around the windows in the kitchen and the door that led to the deck on the side of the house. In the doorway, the sage crackled and flared.

"Does that mean something?" he asked.

"I like to think that the herb is working extra hard to erase whatever happened here. Maybe the couple who lived here before had a fight at this doorway."

While she proceeded through the rest of the downstairs, the smudge stick began to burn low. She placed it in the lotus bowl, and waved her hand to waft the smoke into the corners of the rooms. As she did so, she explained, "Bad energy accumulates in the corners. It gets trapped there and hangs around."

"I can buy that. It's a matter of geometry."

In the upstairs, she went through the same process. In his bedroom, where he hadn't yet unpacked many of the boxes, the sage sputtered wildly at the door to his closet. She took a backward step. "Yikes, I wonder what happened there."

"I know what it is." He stepped through the open closet door, reached up to the top shelf and took down a locked metal box. "My guns are in here. Negative energy?"

"Undoubtedly." His weapons were tools of violence. Even when he was fighting to protect the innocent, the guns represented hurt and pain. "A warrior needs to work extra hard to keep himself in balance."

"Am I a warrior?" He grinned as he replaced his gun box on the shelf. "I'd like that."

She remembered the way he attacked the thug who was trying to hurt Miguel's mother. Brady had been selfless in battle. "I might call you a warrior hero."

"And what should I call you? Are you the yin to my yang?"

She immediately visualized the yin-yang symbol—a circle divided by a curving line with one half black and the other white and a dot on each side. The image fit their relationship. Even though they were opposites, they complemented each other and fit together. In effect, they had joined forces to make a more complete whole.

She'd already consented to be his fake bride, but she wasn't sure that she wanted to be joined in any other way. "Let's finish the smudging."

In her bedroom, she smudged the windows and the doorways. The sage was burning low. "That's it. I'm done."

"Can I add something of my own?"

There was the distinct possibility that he'd pull some kind of wise-guy stunt. "You're asking me to trust you."

He held out his hand. "Give me the lotus bowl."

Her fake wedding band glimmered as she passed the still smoking bowl to him. "Be careful."

"Why?"

"Those ashes could flare up. The spark could ignite and we'd burn the house down, which would be seriously bad juju."

His large hands closed around the edges of the green bowl. He raised it over his head and swept in a slow arc, leaving a fragrant, wispy trail of smoke. Lowering the bowl, he held it between them and gazed across the rim at her.

His voice was a whisper. "While we live in this house, may our minds be wise and our actions be strong."

His sincerity was evident. His words hit her straight in the heart. "I can't believe you did that."

He carried the lotus bowl to her dresser and set it down beside her crystal dolphin. "To be real honest, I can't believe it, either."

"Thank you."

She rested her hand on his shoulder, and he turned toward her. Rising up on tiptoe, she leaned closer to give him a friendly peck on the cheek. That wasn't what happened. She found herself kissing him on the mouth.

Two thoughts occurred simultaneously. Number one: she was surprised. Number two: she liked it.

Petra should have pulled away. Their relationship was complicated enough without adding physical intimacy. But his kiss felt so good, so much better than a dream fantasy. His firm lips exerted a steady pressure against hers. His arm wrapped around her waist and cinched her close. She could feel her heart beating wildly against his lean, muscular chest. Ripples of awareness wakened and elevated her senses to a level that she'd never felt before. His kiss took her beyond excitement and straight into arousal. Her sacral chakra, just below her belly button, radiated with a glowing, all-consuming passion.

When he loosened his grasp, she clung more tightly. *Not yet. Don't stop.* She never wanted this unexpected moment to end. Half in a daze, her eyelids slowly lifted.

She saw fire, her worst fear. Bright yellow flames licked the air.

Immediately, she broke away from him.

The smudge stick in her lotus bowl had flared with a small light, no bigger than her thumb. She stared, uncomprehending. She'd seen an inferno. Now, it was only a spark.

For sure, this was an omen.

THE NEXT MORNING, BRADY groped the bedside table, trying to find his wristwatch before he remembered that he didn't wear a watch, anymore. Nor did he have an alarm clock. He groaned. His undercover identity was damn inconvenient.

And he wasn't doing it very well. Last night when Petra had brushed her sweet lips against his, he hadn't been able to resist, *even though he knew better*. He'd held her against him and had taken his time kissing her back, tasting the honey warmth of her lips and inhaling the musky fragrance of the sage smoke.

At first, she'd fluttered in his arms like a captured hummingbird, and then she'd subsided, relaxing into his embrace as though she belonged there. Her slender, supple body draped around him. Her legs molded against him. Her subtle, natural motions had driven him crazy.

Lying alone in his bed, he reveled in the memory of their kiss. He relived the unbelievable excitement…and the regret. He shouldn't have kissed her, shouldn't have allowed their embrace to continue for more than a few seconds. What the hell was wrong with him? He never lost control.

If he'd believed in magic, he would have assumed that her ritual ceremony had cast a spell over him. When she first started waving her smudge stick, he'd been ready to dismiss her as a superstitious nutcake. But he couldn't fault her motives, and much of what she said made sense. As he followed her from room to room, he found himself agreeing with her. It was emotionally healthy to start in a new place with a fresh attitude.

He didn't know what had startled her. When she

broke contact with him, she didn't give an explanation. All she did was gather up her lotus bowl and tell him that she'd dispose of the ashes.

He'd gone back to his unpacking and had stayed up until two in the morning, putting the house in order. Damn it, what time was it? Morning light spilled around the edges of the window shades, but he couldn't guess the hour.

There was a clock downstairs on the stove. He dragged himself out of bed and grabbed a pair of gray sweatpants from a hook in the closet. He stuck his arms into a plaid flannel bathrobe and tied it around his middle to ward off the morning chill.

Halfway down the staircase, he smelled coffee. Petra had gotten out of bed before him, which was kind of a surprise because she'd described herself as a night owl. He made a beeline to the kitchen. The stove clock said it was seven thirty-nine. Excellent! He required precisely five and a half hours of sleep to function at peak efficiency.

He poured black coffee into a blue mug that he'd washed last night and put away in the wall cabinet to the right of the sink. After taking his first sip, he noticed Petra's matching mug on the countertop. Where was she? If she'd taken off somewhere without consulting him, he'd be seriously annoyed. At the moment, it didn't appear that they were in danger, but they were dealing with serious criminals and had to take precautions.

What they really needed was to come up with a plan. Even though she seemed to be comfortable diving into the unknown, he knew better. Their efforts would be maximized if they had clear objectives. Where the hell was she? He strode across the living room and looked through the front window. The truck was parked where he'd left it, and the dead bolt on the front door was still fastened. She hadn't exited this way.

He returned to the kitchen. The side door leading onto the deck had a window. Pushing aside the curtain, he peeked through the glass. With her back to him, Petra stood on her turquoise yoga mat and balanced on one leg like a crane. Her hair spilled past her shoulders in a wavy curtain of auburn and gold.

Instead of interrupting, he watched as she moved gracefully through different yoga positions, asanas she called them. Her black pants skimmed her legs and outlined her bottom. On top, she wore a fitted, deep purple shirt with flowing sleeves. With her back arched and her arms spread wide, she seemed to be welcoming the sun from the east. He didn't know the correct form, but he admired the way she moved. It was a stretch to think of these slow transitions from one pose to another as exercise. At the same time, he was fairly sure that he couldn't hold one leg behind himself and stretch the opposite arm out straight.

When he stepped outside onto the deck, she continued the motion she'd started, ending with her palms together in a prayerful pose. She nodded her head in a slight bow. "Namaste."

"Right back at you."

Her cheeks were flushed and her blue eyes sparkled. "Is the coffee okay?"

"It's good." He wanted to add that she was also good and beautiful and a pleasure to wake up to. But compliments would lead down a path that he needed to avoid. "How come you're up so early?"

She shrugged. "Maybe I'm changing. You know, becoming more of an early bird to catch the worm."

"I doubt that." He couldn't take his eyes off her. This wasn't good. If he kept staring, he'd want to touch. Gruffly, he said, "We need a plan for today."

"You're right." She squatted and rolled up her yoga mat. "I can wrangle my way back into Lost Lamb by saying I want to check on Dee. But how are we going to get you inside?"

"I could be your assistant."

"Um, no. Nobody will believe that, and I wouldn't be much of a midwife if I needed my husband to hold my hand."

He had given some thought to his way in. "I can say that I want to use some of the women as models."

"Didn't I already shoot down that line?" She sat back on her heels. "And what happens when you actually have to produce a sketch?"

"I can draw some."

"We might be able to come up with some kind of excuse about having you pick me up. Something about the car."

Speaking of which, he heard the sound of tires crunching on gravel. "Somebody's coming."

She bounced to her feet and dashed to the edge of the deck to peer around the corner of the house. "It's a van. I think Margaret is driving."

Before eight o'clock in the morning? It was way too early for another unexpected turn of events. He needed more time to map out their plans. Last night, he should have been working on strategy instead of putting stuff away.

Whirling, she faced him. "I know exactly what we should do. Take off your bathrobe."

"What?"

"You heard me. Margaret has a crush on you. If you give her something to look at, she'll agree to anything."

Her reasoning was shaky at best, but he didn't have any other ideas. He unfastened the tie on his bathrobe and went back into the house to open the front door.

Chapter Nine

Petra knew she'd made the right call when she saw the expression on Margaret's face. The thin young woman stood in their doorway, peering through her long bangs with adoring eyes, clearly mesmerized by the sight of half-naked Brady. Petra couldn't blame her. The man was definitely something to look at, even from the back, *especially* from the back. She noticed a couple of scars across his shoulders, a reminder that he was more than a pretty boy. His body was rugged, lean and muscular. His sweat pants hung low on his hips.

Her supposed husband was innately sexy. Her husband? She felt a pop of jealousy as she joined him at the front door. "Hi, Margaret. Would you like to come in?"

Her small hands twisted in a knot below her chin. "Sorry for coming over so early."

"Is there some kind of problem?" Brady asked. "I sure hope there's nothing wrong."

Petra noticed that when he was playing his undercover role, his slight Texas accent became a more pronounced twang. "Margaret? Is this about Dee?"

"Yes." Margaret inhaled a deep breath and pulled herself together. "Dee is acting like a diva. Even though her water broke, I don't think she's really and truly in labor."

"How far apart are the contractions?"

"They come and go. Have you ever heard of anything like that?"

Petra nodded. "Actually, I have."

"Somehow, Dee got it into her head that she wants you to deliver her baby. Miss Francine sent me to get you."

This invitation was the perfect opportunity to investigate at Lost Lamb. Dee could be in labor for hours, which meant Petra had a reason to hang around, talking to the other women and exploring the facility. "Give me a minute to change clothes, and I'll come back with you."

"Whoa, there," Brady said. He was playing the Texan card as though it was the final draw to a royal flush. "Patty, darlin', remember what we were talking about? About how much I wanted to sketch these ladies?"

"Of course, I do." She immediately understood his ploy. He was fishing for a reason to get himself inside the Lost Lamb. "I remember. Darlin'."

He focused his charm offensive on Margaret

as he explained, "Last night, when I saw all you beautiful ladies, yourself included…"

She giggled like a little girl.

"…I was inspired," he said. "I was hoping some of you would sit for portraits. If I drive over with Patty, I might be able to chat with Miss Francine and get her permission."

"She'll never say yes."

"That's because she hasn't seen how good I am." When he touched Margaret's arm to guide her toward the staircase, she quivered all over. "Come with me. I want to show you some of my paintings."

Petra fought the urge to roll her eyes. Oldest line in the book! But Margaret didn't think so. Eagerly, she ascended the staircase and allowed him to escort her into the back bedroom where he'd set up his studio.

This would be the first time Petra had viewed the art that was supposedly done by Brady Gilliam, and she was curious to see what the *real* Brady had picked from the FBI's stockpile of confiscated paintings. He was such a rational thinker that she couldn't imagine him choosing anything abstract or modernist. If he stayed true to his fed persona, every picture would be black and white with nary a shade of gray.

She couldn't have been more wrong.

Morning light poured through the east window

and splashed against a large canvas that depicted a little girl with black hair playing hide-and-seek, peeking through the limbs of bright yellow forsythia bush. The painting told a story. This little girl didn't beam like a rosy-cheeked cherub. Her mouth was set and determined. Her dark eyes were furtive. It made Petra wonder what the child was hiding from.

Brady showed Margaret around, flipping through canvases stacked against the wall and spreading out pencil sketches on a work table. As far as Petra could tell, all the artwork was portraiture. She wanted to take a more in-depth look, but she couldn't act like this was the first time she'd seen these pictures.

Margaret glanced over her shoulder at her. "I don't see any drawings of you."

Brady explained, "I did a million pictures of Patty when we first met. A lot of them sold. These are my more recent projects."

"Well, they're beautiful," Margaret said. "I'd like for you to do my son. He's three."

"I'd be delighted. And do you think Miss Francine might see fit to let me sketch you ladies?"

She rested her thin hand on his bare bicep. "No harm in asking."

"That's good, real good." He caught her hand and gave a squeeze. "You head back over to the

Lost Lamb. We'll get dressed and be right behind you."

"I don't think so," she said. "Miss Francine won't be happy if I come back without Patty."

Petra wondered if Francine had an ulterior motive in sending Margaret to fetch them. She might be here to check out their story and make sure they were who they said they were. That could be a problem. It was obvious that she and Brady had slept in different bedrooms last night.

"Here's an idea," she said. "Brady can take you downstairs and get you a cup of coffee while I get ready. When we're both dressed, we'll follow you in the truck."

Brady steered her quickly toward the staircase. As soon as they were gone, Petra dashed into her bedroom and made the bed. If anybody asked, she'd say this was the guest room.

She dived into an old pair of jeans. Her purple shirt and sports bra were okay for the top. No time for a shower. She splashed water on her face and yanked her hair into a knot on the top of her head. In less than eight minutes, she descended the staircase, carrying a large backpack filled with a variety of items she used when delivering babies.

As Brady went past her, he whispered, "Don't leave her alone. I don't trust her."

Petra joined Margaret who stood behind the

counter in the kitchen, sipping her coffee. Even though Margaret seemed too timid to be spying on them, there was a calculated look in her eyes as she studied the kitchen. "You must have worked late last night. Everything is put away."

"Brady did most of the work," she said truthfully. "He likes to settle in."

She glanced at the countertop. "Lots of small appliances. Do you enjoy cooking?"

"Not so much." During the drive, she and Brady had discussed this part of their relationship. "I try, but my husband is the real chef in the family."

"That's what he said, too."

Good, their stories agreed. "Cooking is just another way he can be creative."

"You're so lucky to have a man like him." Margaret sighed. "An artist."

"That's not all he does. He's also a fine auto mechanic."

She had the urge to babble on and on about Brady, but he'd warned her that one danger in establishing a cover story was saying too much. Every embellishment had to be remembered.

To avoid getting herself into trouble, she turned the focus around. "Tell me about your son."

Her plain features brightened. "His name is Jeremy, after my dad who passed away when I was four years old. At least, that's what my mom told me. He might have run off with another woman."

Yet, she'd named her son after the father who abandoned her. Margaret must really be yearning for a family connection. "Are there other kids at Lost Lamb that your little boy can play with?"

"He doesn't need anybody but me."

Petra wasn't sure she agreed with that philosophy, but she'd never criticize another woman's child-rearing technique unless there was harm to the child. "I'm sure you're a good mom."

"Jeremy is very bright. Miss Francine says so. She said we should tutor him ourselves instead of sending him to preschool next year."

Brady came racing down the staircase wearing jeans and a San Francisco Giants T-shirt with a lightweight black jacket. Even though he'd thrown himself together and his stubble was thick and his hair uncombed, he looked neat. His personal style simply wasn't going to change. Brady would never be a laid-back artist.

And she decided that was okay with her. His precise personality was reflected in the details of those paintings he'd chosen to represent himself.

DURING THE BRIEF DRIVE to the Lost Lamb Ranch, Brady tried to hammer one important concept into Petra's head. While she was there, she had to maintain their cover. "Don't investigate. Take no risks."

"I'll be careful," she promised.

"Let me repeat. Take no risks. If Francine gets suspicious or figures out that we're investigating, the whole operation could disappear. Those pregnant women would be swept into more danger than they're in right now. Do you understand?"

"I get it." She threw up her hands in a gesture that was both annoying and graceful. "By the way, the paintings supposedly done by Brady Gilliam are really wonderful. How does the FBI come up with stuff like that?"

He'd explain his artwork later. Right now, he wanted her to focus on just one thing. "Let's be completely clear. No snooping. No asking of probing questions. No eavesdropping."

"If I'm not investigating, what should I do?"

"Observe," he said. "Don't search for evidence. Let them show it to you."

"And if I happen to run across something?"

"Call me on my cell phone," he said. "Lost Lamb is the best lead we've uncovered in the human trafficking network. This could be our only chance to get to the people at the top."

"Like the lawyer in Durango," she said.

"He's another lead."

From his prior research, Brady didn't think Stan Mancuso ranked among the upper echelon of the organization. No doubt, he was taking a payoff to handle paperwork, but he wasn't making a million-dollar profit. Nor did Francine Kelso seem like one of the big fish.

He parked the truck beside Margaret's van, and they followed her into the house where she escorted them into Francine's office to the left of the front foyer—a high-ceiling room with a dark cherry desk and a fancy rug with a maroon-and-blue detailing. The walls were plain white, but the fancy antique furniture reminded him of an old-fashioned bordello. A couple of cheap Degas prints hung on the wall in ornate frames.

Francine stood behind her desk. She wore a black silk kimono embroidered with colorful dragons. Even though it was before nine o'clock in the morning, she was already in full makeup. Her dark Cleopatra eyes regarded him dismissively as she spoke to Petra. "Dee wants you to deliver her baby. How much is this going to cost me?"

"I have a sliding scale," Petra said. "I prefer an integrated, holistic approach to childbirth. That includes prenatal exercise, the birth itself and postpartum instruction."

"None of these girls need postpartum." Francine gestured for them to sit opposite her desk. "These babies are being given up for adoption."

"Having the baby adopted doesn't mean the mom is immune to postpartum depression," Petra said. "It's partly a matter of hormonal imbalance, and can be incredibly detrimental to the mother's emotional and physical health."

"Not my problem. I take care of them until after the baby is born, then they're on their own."

Her expression was Arctic cold, but Brady wasn't here to judge. He opened a notebook-size sketch pad and took out a pencil. The ornate picture frames on the wall gave him reason to hope that Francine might be interested in having her portrait done. If she agreed to sit for him, he had an in.

While the two women wrangled over the cost of Petra's services, he sketched a flattering rendition of Francine's dark eyes and shining black hair. He made sure to include her cleavage and one of her manicured hands.

"Excuse me," she snapped at him. "What the hell are you doing?"

He met her gaze and smiled. "I'm an artist. While we were at the house, Margaret saw some of my work and can vouch for me."

"Margaret isn't qualified as an art critic. Are you drawing pictures? Of what?"

"Of you. You have a striking bone structure. I want to paint you." He handed over the sketch book with her picture. "I could do an oil portrait for your office."

Petra leaned forward to catch a glimpse of his pencil drawing. "Wow," she said.

Francine fired a sharp gaze in her direction. "You sound surprised."

"That's one of the best first sketches I've ever seen my husband do. He must really be inspired."

"It is rather good." She held up the picture and looked at one of the frames on the wall. "You're an expensive couple to know. How much do you charge for a portrait?"

"My art isn't about money," he said. "I'd like to do three or four sittings with you, and then finish up the details at my home studio. When I'm done, you pay me what you think the painting is worth."

"Not much of a businessman, are you? You're lucky to have a wife who works." She circled her desk until she was standing in front of him. Purposefully seductive, she perched on the edge of her desk. Her kimono fell open, exposing her long legs which she crossed. "I hope you get your money's worth, Patty."

"I do," Petra said. "Brady has many talents."

"Such as?"

"For one thing, he's a terrific chef."

"I'll bet."

She lowered her gaze to focus on his crotch. This was a challenge. He thought it was less about sex than about power. She wanted to put him in his place.

In his undercover identity as a laid-back artist, he might have backed down. But his instincts wouldn't let him. She wanted to play games. *Fine with me. Bring it on.*

He rose to his feet. His gaze locked with hers. "Do you see anything you like?"

"I believe I do." She placed the sketchpad in his hands. "We have a deal, Brady. Our first sitting will be at two o'clock this afternoon."

"You won't be disappointed."

She got off the desk and turned to Petra. "I'm going to hire you, too. If things work out well with Dee, I might put you on retainer. Margaret will show you where to find Dee."

Petra asked, "Is she in the room where we were before?"

"Certainly not. I can't have the other girls being disturbed. Women in labor are loud. They have to be removed from the house."

Her disgust was evident. Brady figured she couldn't care less about the other pregnant women. It was Francine herself who didn't want her day disrupted by inconvenient screams of pain. A true sociopath, she had less empathy than a predator shark circling her prey.

Dealing with her wouldn't be easy. He'd have to be on guard. Painting her without fangs and devil horns would be a real challenge.

Chapter Ten

On the veranda outside the front door of the Lost Lamb, Petra went up on tiptoe to give Brady a wifely kiss on the cheek. Thoughts of what had happened last night when she attempted the same maneuver were a million miles away. They were in enemy territory, and she didn't dare lose control.

Ignoring his masculine scent and the heat that radiated from him, she whispered, "Nice job with the dominatrix, Picasso."

"Be careful," he responded.

There was much she wanted to talk with him about, starting with his artistic talent. His quick sketch of Francine was the same style as the paintings at the house. He was the artist—a biographical detail she never would have guessed. She'd pegged him as a guy who loved the rules—not someone who enjoyed coloring outside the lines.

Margaret joined them. Her smile was meant only for Brady. "Congratulations," she said.

"Francine doesn't hire just anybody. She likes the best of the best."

Or the cheapest. Petra was certain that his offer to charge only what Francine wanted to pay had clinched the deal. "I hope she won't be disappointed by either of us."

"We'll see." Margaret scowled at her. "Come with me. I'll show you where Dee is."

"I need my backpack from the truck. I brought along a few things that are helpful in childbirth."

"We have all the medical equipment."

"And I'm sure it's state-of-the-art," Petra said as she left the veranda and went toward the truck. "But I like my own stethoscope and fetal monitor."

Margaret glanced over her shoulder as though she was considering running back to the house to ask Francine's permission.

Brady touched her arm and changed her mind. "My wife is real stubborn about having her own things while she's working. I promise there's nothing to fret about."

"I suppose it's all right."

At the truck, Brady opened the passenger door and reached inside for the extra-large backpack she'd stowed under the dashboard. "I'll carry this for you."

"You can't come with us," Margaret said nervously.

"I won't be in the way," he promised.

"Sorry, but nobody is allowed."

Petra knew why Brady had offered to be her pack mule. He wanted to see where they were headed. Earlier, he'd told her not to investigate, not under any circumstance. Now that they were here, in the heart of the Lost Lamb, he was tempted.

So far, they'd been lucky. Francine had hired both of them. They had an in. The smart move was to avoid anything that might be considered suspicious. She took the backpack from him and hoisted it onto her shoulders. "It's okay, Brady. I'll give you a call if anything comes up."

"Let's go," Margaret said. She tilted her head up for another longing gaze at Brady. "Goodbye. For now."

As Petra fell into step beside Margaret, she didn't look back at Brady. She was on her own and needed to focus, to observe and to draw conclusions. The investigation had begun.

The end goal was to figure out who was behind the baby trafficking operation and to get evidence to arrest them. But she'd start with a smaller objective. If Lost Lamb was a front for a bigger operation, she suspected that there were more than five pregnant women involved. Who were they? Where were they being held?

Behind the main house were two long bunkhouses painted gray with sloping roofs in a rusty red that matched the roof on the two-story main house. Margaret led her along a wide, asphalt path toward the bunkhouse on the left. None of the other pathways around the house were paved. Petra asked, "Is this a road?"

"If one of the women in labor has complications, we need to be able to get an ambulance down here to pick her up."

A paved road would also be useful for dropping off human cargo. In front of the bunkhouse was an asphalt area with enough room for a truck to make a turnaround. Not a bad setup for a smuggling operation. Vehicles pulling in and out would make aerial surveillance difficult, especially at night.

Petra asked, "How many people live at Lost Lamb?"

"Miss Francine is in the house, of course. Then, there's me and my little boy—"

"Jeremy," Petra supplied his name.

"That's right. Jeremy and I have a bedroom and playroom in the main house. Robert and the other handymen are in that bunkhouse." She pointed. "The pregnant girls come and go, of course. There are usually three or four of them."

"And they have bedrooms in the house?"

"That's right."

"What about this bunkhouse?" she asked. "Who lives here?"

"The birthing room is at the end, and it's separate. The other part is arranged like a barrack with cots on both sides. Usually, there's nobody staying there."

The windows on the bunkhouse were shuttered. A shiny padlock fastened the door at the far end. Petra would like to get inside and look around.

Margaret opened the door to the separate room, and they walked inside. The birthing suite—consisting of a bedroom, a delivery room and a bathroom—was surprisingly pleasant. In the bedroom, the sunlight from two windows dappled the pale yellow walls and filtered through light blue drapes. The color scheme reminded her of Miguel's baby blanket.

Dee sprawled in the double bed, sleeping. In a padded chair beside her, a pregnant woman with a long brown braid flipped through a fashion magazine, no doubt dreaming of the day when she could wear skinny jeans again. Disinterested, she looked up. "About time. I've been here forever."

Petra introduced herself, thinking that she might be delivering this woman's baby within the week. She asked, "How's Dee been doing?"

"Not so hot. She said she was hungry but didn't eat any of the breakfast I brought her." She pointed to a tray by the door with a napkin draped over it. "She didn't puke, though."

Petra could smell the grease from sausage patties and congealed eggs. Not appetizing in the least. She went to the bed and lightly stroked the blond hair off Dee's forehead. Her skin was pinkish and warm but not feverish. "How long has she been sleeping?"

"Half an hour."

Petra glanced back and forth between the pregnant woman and Margaret. Their faces were blank. They had very little idea about how to take care of a woman in labor or how to make her comfortable. "Who delivers the babies?"

Margaret answered, "Miss Francine is a nurse, but she has somebody she calls."

"A doctor?"

"He shows up when the contractions are a couple of minutes apart."

Before this supposed doctor arrived, the expectant mothers were on their own, facing an intense experience with minimal support. Petra's protective instincts rose to the surface. These women shouldn't be treated so coldly. Giving birth should be a wonderful experience.

"I can take care of Dee from here," she said. "If either of you would like to learn about birthing techniques, I'd be happy to show you."

Margaret held up her palm, warding off the suggestion. "I have other chores to do."

"Been there, done that." The pregnant woman pointed to her belly. "This is my third."

She didn't look older than twenty. Her arms and legs were thin. Her complexion pale. In an authoritative voice, Petra said, "You should be eating leafy green veggies. Are you taking prenatal vitamins as well as calcium and iron?"

"It's too many pills. They make me nauseous."

"The vitamins are as much for you as for the baby." Hadn't anyone bothered to talk to her about these things? "Your body is providing fuel for the baby to grow. It's important to take care of your nutrition. If you don't have enough calcium, it could lead to problems with bone density."

"I'm fine."

A young woman like her wouldn't be concerned with osteoporosis, but Petra knew how to get her attention. "You could lose your hair. Your fingernails will be brittle, and you could get acne."

"Okay, okay, I'll take the pills."

"And eat the veggies."

"Whatever."

She and Margaret fled from the room in a hurry. And Petra turned her full attention to Dee who was sleeping fitfully. No wonder Dee had wanted to see her. Margaret and these other women didn't know how to take care of her. And Francine—if she really was a nurse—didn't want to be bothered.

When Dee opened her eyes, a tear slipped from

the corner. "I've been thinking about my baby. My son. I want to do what's right for him."

Earlier, Dee had been anxious to be dosed with drugs, shove the baby out and get on with her life. Being close to the time of delivery had changed her attitude. "You want a more natural delivery."

"That's your thing, isn't it? As a midwife?"

"I want what's best for you. And for your son." She sat on the edge of the bed and held Dee's hand. "Tell me about your contractions."

"It's like cramps. Comes and goes in waves."

"Let's see what we can do to make you feel better. First, I'll do a quick examination to see how far along you are in the labor."

Dee sat up on the bed. "Do you want me on the examination table?"

Adjoining the pleasant little bedroom was a more sterile delivery room and a table with stirrups. Convenient for examinations, but Petra preferred for Dee to be comfortable. "I can examine you right here. Let me get my stuff from the backpack."

"You're so nice," Dee said. "Everybody around here is so mean. If I'd known they were going to be so nasty, I never would have agreed to any of this. It was my boyfriend's idea."

"It usually is."

Petra unloaded some of her equipment on a long countertop against the back wall. In addition to her medical supplies, she had incense and candles, herbal tea, cozy wool socks, a pair of scrubs for herself, a soft blanket for the mom and a player for digital music. The whole idea was to nurture Dee and help her relax into the natural process.

"It's not his baby," Dee said.

Petra needed to be careful about what she said. Even though they seemed to be alone, this room could be bugged. "It's okay, Dee. The only thing you need to think about is having this baby."

"My baby. Mine. It's my egg."

That was an odd phrase. "Are you trying to tell me something?"

"I don't even know the father." The whining tone was back in her voice. "I'm a surrogate."

BEING UNDERCOVER WAS one thing. Not using the resources available to him as an FBI agent was another. In his art studio at the house, Brady hooked up his laptop computer with a wide screen monitor and a laser printer as he considered his options. He could call for a chopper or request backup, thereby ending their undercover operation.

Electronic surveillance was more subtle. If he'd been thinking more clearly this morning, he would have taken a bug with him to leave in Francine's office or fitted Petra with a two-way communication device that allowed him to hear every word she said. Who was she talking to?

What was she saying? Did they suspect her? His gut wrenched when he thought of her inside that place, alone.

How much longer before his two o'clock appointment with Francine? He automatically checked his wrist. No watch, damn it. He logged on to the computer to check the time stamp. Ten thirty-five. Three and a half hours from now until he'd return to the Lost Lamb.

Fighting his rising tension, he inhaled and exhaled a couple of deep breaths, catching a whiff of the burned sage she used in smudging. If anything bad happened to her...

Focus on the positive. He had three and a half hours, plenty of time to do something. Maybe he should go on foot and explore the terrain surrounding the ranch in case they needed escape routes. But skulking around was risky; Robert or one of the other handymen might notice him. If he was seen, his cover was blown.

Thus far, their plan had worked to perfection. Getting invited into Lost Lamb had been easy. Too easy? Were they falling into a trap? Realistically, he doubted it. Francine had no reason to suspect that she was being investigated. When he and Petra showed up, they appeared to be newcomers to the area who were looking for work. Their story about inheriting a house was believable, and the FBI paperwork validating his ownership would stand up to computer scrutiny.

Brady knew that his plan to introduce a midwife into a supposed home for unwed mothers was solid. Francine *wanted* to believe Petra was who she said she was—Patty Gilliam, his wife.

When Margaret showed up this morning, he realized that their house didn't exactly fit the cover story. She'd noticed that he didn't have sketches of Petra—a lapse on his part. He should have thought of that. And they didn't have photos of themselves together. No wedding photos.

A task presented itself. He wasn't a computer genius, but he could photoshop digital pictures to create a composite of their life together. Without too much effort, he hacked into Petra's personal files and started going through her photos.

Lucky for him, there were several pictures of her in San Francisco from a recent trip to visit her family. She wasn't always laughing or smiling in these snapshots, but her presence was compelling. His eye went directly to her.

One picture caught his eye. She stood alone on a rocky beach. The wind blew her hair back, and her delicate profile was outlined against the dark waters of the Pacific. She seemed to be seeing something remarkable. Carefully, he added a photo of himself to the setting, creating a memory that didn't really exist.

When his cell phone rang, he jumped. The caller ID said Patty. He answered quickly but was careful to keep his voice calm. "Hi, there, darlin'. How are you doing?"

"Just fine." She matched his fake calm with her own brand of easygoing serenity. "I wanted to let you know about Dee. She's twenty percent effaced and dilated to three centimeters."

He didn't know if that was good news or bad. "How long until the baby comes?"

"That's something I need to talk to her about."

He heard music in the background. *Hello, Dolly?* "Sounds like you're having a party."

"You know me," she said. "Bringing a new life into the world is cause for celebration."

"I'm going to be there at two. Is there anything I can bring for you?"

"As a matter of fact, there is. Because we don't have much food in the house, you should go to the diner in Kirkland for lunch. Hold on a second."

He heard her conferring with Dee.

Petra came back on the phone. "The diner is called Royal Burger. And Dee wants a strawberry milkshake. Could you pick one up and bring it back here?"

"No problem."

Dee was talking in the background, interrupting. Petra responded to her before she said, "Somebody told Dee that women in labor aren't supposed to eat anything. Recent studies indicate that it doesn't make a difference. I mean, I wouldn't recommend a T-bone and fries, but a milkshake is okay."

He fought the urge to yell. *Are you all right? Are you safe?* The latest midwife bulletin on diet and birthing wasn't something he gave a damn about. "See you later," he muttered.

"Take care, darlin'."

His frustration at standing outside and watching Petra take all the risk was killing him. Undercover work wasn't his thing. He needed a straightforward course of action with a clear objective. He needed to be in charge.

Before he left the house, he gathered up the necessary art supplies for his sitting with Francine. In the secret pocket of his backpack, he hid electronic devices—bugs, mini-cams and GPS trackers. *Do I have a plan for what I'll do with these things? Not a clue, but at least I'm prepared.*

Grabbing the keys to the truck, he proceeded onward to his assignment. Go to Royal Burger and get a strawberry milkshake. What a total waste of his FBI training and eight years of experience as a special agent.

The drive to Kirkland took less than fifteen minutes. Although Royal Burger wasn't on the main drag, he found it easily. A tour of the entire town wouldn't take more than ten minutes.

Several other vehicles were parked out front. This was his chance to meet the locals. *I'm Brady Gilliam, laid-back artist and car mechanic.* With his stubble, jeans and faded Giants T-shirt, he ought to fit right in.

As soon as he walked through the door, he spotted someone he'd already met. The mountain of a man known as Robert sat at a table with two other guys. Brady waved and went toward him. This trip might prove useful after all.

Chapter Eleven

Petra didn't know what to make of Dee. After her dramatic announcement that she was a surrogate, she'd clammed up—feigning a desperate need for attention and leaving Petra with a lot of questions. If surrogacy was involved in the baby trafficking operation, Francine was working on a more sophisticated level than they'd originally thought. The fees charged for surrogates could be astronomical, and the legality in some states was questionable. As soon as possible, Brady needed to question the lawyer in Durango who handled Lost Lamb's business.

In the meantime, Dee was the main source of information, and she was too busy whining to be useful. Petra helped her into the shower and changed the sheets on her bed and found the show tunes music she'd said she liked. After Dee was cozy and calm, Petra did a standard examination. That was when she discovered that Dee the Diva was a liar.

After fluffing the pillows behind Dee's back, Petra asked, "When was your last contraction?"

"A little while ago."

"Was it when I was checking your baby's heartbeat with the fetal monitor?"

"Right."

She was pretty when she smiled. Her full cheeks were rosy, and her eyes were a compelling though somewhat vapid blue. If the choice of egg donor was based on attractiveness and health, Dee made a good candidate. Intelligence was another matter. She wasn't even clever enough to lie successfully.

"If the contraction came when I was touching you," Petra said, "I should have felt it. And I didn't."

"Well, it might have been a different time. Like when I was in the shower."

"Did you hear what I said to Brady on the phone?"

"About my milkshake?"

"About your examination. You're ten percent effaced and dilated to three centimeters."

Dee shrugged. "What does that mean?"

"You're not in labor."

"Oh, yes, I am."

"Labor doesn't really get started until you're around five centimeters. Hard labor comes when you're eight to ten. And you need to be one-hundred-percent effaced to deliver. And, by the way, your water hasn't broken."

"You can tell that?"

"Here's a bit of free advice," Petra said. "If you're going to lie, you need to know the facts. You haven't even bothered to learn the basics of pregnancy and delivery."

"I should be in labor." Her hands drew into tight little fists. Petulant as a child, she pounded the covers. "My due date was four days ago."

"Why should I believe you? Everything you've told me is phony." Digging for information, she said, "And you expect me to believe you're a surrogate? Ha!"

"That's true," Dee protested.

"Prove it. Tell me how you got pregnant."

"My boyfriend signed me up, and we got paid two hundred dollars. I took these pills that made me produce extra eggs, and then I went to this doctor and he gave me a pelvic exam and harvested the eggs." She paused for a proud smile. "He said I was one of the most fertile women he'd ever seen."

She continued with a description of in vitro insemination that was accurate enough to convince Petra that Dee had gone through the process. According to her, she and her boyfriend had been paid two thousand dollars so far. After the baby was delivered, she'd be paid another three thousand. The payoff was pathetic, considering that the typical cost for a surrogate birth was twenty times that much.

Petra asked, "Why did you tell me all those other lies?"

"When I met you and Brady on the road, I just wanted to get Margaret off my back. She's been pestering me to hurry up and have the baby. That's why I faked having my water break."

"How did you pull that off?"

"Nothing to it," Dee said. "When you were all looking the other way, I emptied a water bottle between my legs. I was already planning to do it with Margaret. Having you and Brady show up was icing on the cupcake."

"Didn't you know that once the water broke, you'd be expected to start labor?"

"Don't be mad at me." She flopped back against the pillows. "You're the only person who has been nice. And I liked what you said about having a baby. It makes me special. I want to do it right. The natural way."

"Even if it hurts?"

"There aren't many things I'm good at," Dee said. "But I'm super-fertile and had an easy pregnancy. I might have a talent for this birth stuff."

Petra didn't want to be sympathetic to this lying little diva, but her need to be special was both sad and touching. "I'm sure you'll be a star."

"I can maybe even be a good mom," Dee said. "I don't have any family except for my boyfriend. I haven't heard from him since I got here."

"When was that?"

"Three weeks ago." Her lower lip pushed out in a pout. "Francine took my cell phone away. She said it was better if I didn't talk to anybody until after the baby was born."

Cutting off communication was probably a tactic designed to give Francine control over her herd of pregnant women. They wouldn't have anyone else giving them advice or suggesting that they didn't want to give their babies up for adoption. Francine was the boss, and Petra needed to remember that. Even though she hated the idea of a baby factory, devoid of nurturing for mother or child, she had to stay on Francine's good side. Her undercover job was to deliver the babies. Her investigation was to save them.

And she needed to act fast. Dee wasn't in labor yet, but she would be soon. As would the other women. Petra couldn't stand by and watch while these helpless infants were drawn into unknown circumstances.

The door to the birthing suite swung open, and a bald man with tinted glasses stepped inside. There was nothing unusual about him except for the pristine white lab coat he wore over his khaki trousers and cotton shirt. "I'm Dr. Smith."

He smirked when he said his name. *Dr. Smith? Might as well call him Doc Anonymous.* Petra suspected it was an alias. "I'm surprised to see you, Doctor. I was told that you only showed up in the last stages of labor."

"I came to meet you."

Petra held out her hand. "Patty Gilliam."

His handshake was quick, as though he was protecting his clean, soft hands. And his skin was cold, almost reptilian. "You're a midwife. Correct?"

"A licensed, certified nurse-midwife."

He gestured toward Dee. "Tell me about this one."

"Why don't we step outside for a moment?" She glanced toward Dee. "We'll be right back."

Standing on the asphalt outside the bunkhouse, she pasted a complacent expression on her face. She needed to make nice with Dr. Smith. He was an important part of the investigation—an integral part. He was the one who delivered the babies. Was he a real doctor? An OB-GYN? If so, what happened to his Hippocratic oath to "first do no harm"? Petra was certain that Smith knew about the baby smuggling. Otherwise he wouldn't be using a fake name.

"Do you have a problem?" he asked.

"Me? Not at all." She had to convince him that she wasn't a threat. More than that, she wanted him to trust her enough to put her on retainer so she'd have full and unlimited access to Lost Lamb.

"Why did we come outside to talk?"

"I couldn't speak freely in front of Dee. Here's the thing. She isn't really in labor. I examined her. She's ten percent effaced and dilated three centimeters."

"Coming here was a waste of my time." His skin was pale. His bald head shone as white as a skull. "Damn these girls."

If Petra had been acting like herself, she would have argued that every part of the birthing process—including the to-be-expected weirdness from the mother—deserved attention. But she wouldn't argue with Smith. "You're absolutely right. You shouldn't have been called. I know how important a doctor's time is. That's one of the best reasons for using a midwife."

"Like you?" He managed to imbue those two words with an icy sneer.

"Exactly like me." She lifted a shoulder and tilted her head so she wouldn't appear confrontational. Her body language should be telling him that she was cooperative. "I'd like to work here on a regular basis."

"Tell me about yourself. I suppose you prefer natural childbirth methods."

No way could she lie about this. "I do."

"It's not my preferred method, but there are advantages. With vaginal delivery, the recovery process is more efficient." His tinted lenses darkened in the direct sunlight making it difficult to read his expression. "Did Dee mention that she's a surrogate?"

"As a matter of fact, she did." Petra knew she should tread lightly on this topic. "And I think it's wonderful. A healthy young woman like Dee is an excellent choice for surrogacy. Her blood pressure is normal. The baby's heartbeat is strong. Barring any unforeseen complication, she ought to have a healthy baby."

"And you can deliver the baby without my assistance?"

"Yes, sir."

"A question," he said. "Why did Dee pretend to be in labor?"

"Between you and me," she said with a conspiratorial grin, "she was feeling sorry for herself and wanted to be pampered."

"How do you handle that attitude?"

"By paying a bit of attention to her. I called my husband and asked him to pick up Dee's favorite food—a strawberry milkshake. After she has the milkshake, I'll get her out of bed. If it's all right with you, I'd like to check on her a couple of times a day. That way you won't have to waste your valuable time."

He took a step closer to her. His voice lowered to a whisper so cold that she shivered. "You understand, Patty, that our work here is confidential."

"Absolutely. I might not be a doctor, but I respect patient privilege. I won't talk to anyone." *Except the FBI and maybe local law enforcement.* "May I be honest, Dr. Smith?"

He gave a nod.

"Being so close to the Lost Lamb is like hitting the jackpot for a midwife. From the looks of things, you've got enough pregnant ladies to provide me with steady work. We sure could use the money."

"I don't handle the finances."

Of course not. He wouldn't want to get his delicate hands dirty. "But I'll bet Francine listens to your opinion."

"Yes."

"If you put me on retainer, I could save you a lot of time," she said. "I'm good at my job, and I'm willing to do just about anything to fit in."

"When Dee goes into labor, you'll be called to deliver the baby. If that goes well, we'll consider using your services on a regular basis."

It wasn't as wide an opening as she'd hoped for, but she'd take it. "Thanks so much."

"Carry on," he said.

As he started back toward the house, she spotted Brady coming down the road-size path toward them. Robert was escorting him, and she had the feeling that her milkshake plan had gone sour. All she'd wanted was to see Brady for a couple of minutes to give him an update. Why was Robert tagging along?

She skipped up beside Smith. "That's my husband now."

After she introduced the two men, she took the strawberry milkshake from Brady. "Thanks for getting this. I'll give it to Dee. When you come back this afternoon, I need to take the truck. Okay?"

"Fine with me." He turned on his heel and headed back the way he came. "I'll be going now. Nice to meet you, Doc."

Her exchange with Brady was casual and, apparently, believable. Dr. Smith barely glanced at her supposed husband. And Robert gave him a wave goodbye as though the two of them were on the road to becoming BFFs.

Big Robert came toward her. In his cowboy hat, he looked even more gigantic than last night. His head eclipsed the sun. His voice rumbled. "I'll give the milkshake to Dee."

"The birthing room is private." Petra held on to the tall foam container. "She might not want to see you."

"Are you saying no?"

It probably wasn't a word he heard often. "I'm setting boundaries. When a woman is in labor, she doesn't want to be disturbed."

"Is Dee in labor?"

"No."

"I'll take the milkshake."

She wasn't sure if he intended to be intimidating or if his massive size automatically caused that effect. Either way, she didn't want to argue. She handed him the container. "It looked like you and Brady arrived at the same time."

"Ran into him at Royal Burger," Robert said. "When he told me what he was doing, I got a ride back with him."

"I'm so glad you're getting to know each other. Brady needs to find work other than art."

Robert grunted a noncommittal response. Milkshake in hand, he stalked toward the door to the birthing room. Before he entered, he brushed the dust off his jeans and straightened his collar as though he was a boyfriend picking up his date. It was clear why he wanted to see Dee. He had a crush on her.

Petra had witnessed this phenomenon before. Some men were attracted to pregnant women. The bigger the belly, the harder they fell. She didn't understand but didn't judge.

When Robert opened the door and stepped

inside, she heard Dee squeal. "Robbie! I'm so happy to see you."

Apparently, the attraction went both ways.

Chapter Twelve

Brady arrived ten minutes early for his sitting with Francine, hoping he could catch a moment alone with Petra. They hadn't talked since early this morning, and he wanted to make sure she was all right. The glimpse he'd had when he delivered the milkshake was reassuring, but Dr. Smith worried him.

With his cold manner and white lab coat, Smith didn't fit the stereotype for a crime boss who ran a human trafficking ring. His position in the hierarchy was difficult to deduce. He didn't act like a leader, but he was too cold and arrogant to take orders. Most likely, he worked alone.

In determining a profile, Brady didn't generally use words like creepy or evil, but that was an apt description. As soon as he shook Smith's hand, he knew the guy needed watching.

When Smith entered Lost Lamb, probably to talk to Francine, Brady had taken advantage of the few moments when no one was watching him. His truck was parked beside Smith's SUV. Standing between the two vehicles, Brady had attached a GPS tracker to the driver's-side wheel well of Smith's SUV.

He'd expected to use the tracking device on Robert's vehicle, but he'd revised his opinion of the handyman after their chat at Royal Burger.

The big man was fiercely loyal and proud to be doing his job, which he saw as protecting the women at Lost Lamb. With the right incentive, Robert might become an ally.

Parking the truck outside Lost Lamb, Brady looked for Petra. Instead, he saw Margaret leave the veranda and stroll toward him. She was all smiles, and when she got closer he could tell that she'd put on eye makeup. "Nice to see you, Brady."

"Same here." He climbed out from behind the steering wheel. "Is my wife around? I need to give her the keys to the truck."

"I think she's still with Dee." Margaret held out her hand. "I'll make sure she gets the keys."

He spotted Petra jogging on the wide path that led to the bunkhouse. She was the picture of health. Her stride synchronized perfectly with her arm movement in spite of the large backpack she wore. Her auburn hair fell loosely around her shoulders as she bounced up beside him and planted one of those friendly cheek kisses that were making him hungry for more physical contact.

"You're early," she said.

"Anxious to get started. You know how I am at the start of a new project."

"Planning, planning, planning," she said.

"Are you going to be staying here with Dee?" he asked.

"She doesn't really need me right now, so I'm going home for a while. What time should I come back here to pick you up?"

"You don't have to come back, Patty." Margaret moved closer to him, so close that her shoulder brushed his arm. "I'll give Brady a ride home."

"Wouldn't want you to go to any trouble," he said.

"It's fine. Besides, I want to be alone with you."

"You do?"

She giggled as though he'd said something clever. "I need to talk to you about a portrait of my son."

He'd been doing his best to ignore Margaret's attention, but her approach was becoming aggressive. She'd gone from timid to blatant—rubbing up against him and growling under her breath like a cat in heat.

Petra linked her arm through his. "My husband loves painting children's portraits."

"It's a shame you don't have any kids," Margaret said.

"We will when it's the right time. We agree on everything, don't we, darlin'?"

Standing between these two women, he recalled the talk he and Petra had about jealousy. Though she'd quoted Gandhi, he sensed that she was at least a little bit possessive. Right now, she seemed to be asserting her claim on him. Stroking his arm, she purred, "We're totally on the same page. Aren't we?"

"That's right."

"Surely not," Margaret said. "Brady is an artist. An independent thinker."

"My husband—" Petra emphasized the *my* "—is always thinking. He's full of ideas, and he shares everything with me."

"Do tell."

He was getting the distinct impression that they might each grab an arm and rip him in half. Not that Petra was serious. She was only playing her undercover role as his wife…and giving a damn good performance. If he didn't know better, he'd think she was a jealous wife.

He stepped free from the female sandwich. "I'd better get inside. Something tells me that Francine doesn't like to be kept waiting."

Petra nodded to Margaret. "Please call me on my cell phone if Dee actually goes into labor."

"Sure thing."

After he grabbed his worn leather portfolio from the front seat, he followed Margaret toward the veranda. His plan was to plant a couple of bugs in the house. These high-tech transmitters—about the size of a matchbox—were capable of communicating with the receiver he'd hidden in his home art studio, twelve miles away.

From what he'd seen of the layout on the main floor, the right half of the house was a common area with living room and dining room leading to the kitchen. Margaret directed him to the left, and they entered Francine's office.

Giving him a seductive glance through her lashes, Margaret said, "Patty seemed a little bit upset."

"Did she?"

He wanted to distract Margaret so he could place the listening device. His task was complicated by the possibility that Francine might have surveillance cameras in the office. It seemed likely that she'd want to be able to keep an eye on her charges. Unfortunately, mini-cams were so small that he couldn't hope to spot them without a thorough search.

Margaret whispered, "I don't think Patty appreciates you."

Encouraging her was just plain cruel, but he needed every edge he could get. And he reminded himself that Margaret wasn't a total innocent. She was closely associated with Francine and had to realize that these babies weren't headed toward bona fide adoptions.

He whispered back, "I shouldn't say this about my wife, but you know how it is when you've been married for a while. You start to take each other for granted."

"If I were married to someone like you," she said as she turned to face him, "I'd make you feel special."

He took advantage of her closeness to bump against her and drop his portfolio. Bending down to pick it up, he used a subtle sleight of hand to affix a bug to the bottom side of Francine's desk. Mission accomplished.

A door at the rear of the office pushed open, and Francine stepped through. "What's going on out here?"

"Nothing." Margaret jumped back. "I was escorting Brady here for your sitting, Miss Francine."

"Leave us."

After Margaret had scuttled from the office and closed the door behind her, Francine struck a noble pose. She wore a sleek black wig in a chin-length bob, and she was dressed in equestrian gear—high boots, jodhpurs and a white blouse unbuttoned to show cleavage. Completing the costume, she carried a riding crop. The look was appropriate for a lady of the manor—maybe Lady Chatterley.

"That's a dramatic outfit," he said.

"I might like a portrait with one of the horses."

"Do you ride?"

"Of course." She slapped the crop against her thigh. "Come with me. We're going to the horse barn."

As an artist, he would advise against using the barn for a setting. As an undercover agent, he welcomed the opportunity to check out another building on the property. "Right behind you."

Together, he and Francine trekked across the front yard toward the tall, gray barn. He noted that the double doors were plenty large enough for a semi. If Lost Lamb was a stopping point for human trafficking, a big rig could be hidden here.

Digging for information, he said, "This is quite an operation you've got here."

"My portrait should be classic. Nothing cheap."

"Just what I was thinking."

His smile was wasted on her. Even though Francine radiated sexuality, she wasn't interested in him that way. He figured that she saw people based on how she could use them. His job was to immortalize her in a portrait.

He noticed the track of heavy-duty tires in the dirt outside the barn, which confirmed his earlier suspicion about the big rigs. A couple of days ago, when he'd questioned Miguel's mother, she'd told him that they were transported in a big truck. And she mentioned that one time when they were stopped, she heard horses.

When they entered the barn, two cowboys who had been sitting on a bench leaped into action. Brady recognized them from the Royal Burger, and he called out a greeting.

They gave him a nod but said nothing to Francine as they hustled out an open door at the rear of the barn. Their deference to her made it obvious who was in charge.

She strode to the stalls at the left side of the barn where a well-groomed black stallion nickered a greeting. Francine reached up to stroke his nose and to tell him that he was a good boy. His gleaming coat matched her hair.

"He's a beauty," she said. "If I have him in the portrait, he might draw too much attention away from me."

"It would be a different sort of picture," Brady said. "The barn might not be the best setting. The light in here isn't great."

"What do you suggest? The main thing is that I don't want to look stiff and posed."

He held up his portfolio. "I brought along samples of my work to give you some ideas."

She stalked to a workbench at the rear of the barn and pushed aside the tools littering the tabletop. "Show me."

Before he could spread out his sketches and watercolors, he heard a cough and turned toward the sound. In a darkened corner of the barn, he saw two pregnant women. He'd seen one of them last night. He recognized the other from her photo in the Missing Persons file.

According to information from Cole, this girl had disappeared from the streets of Denver. If she'd been kidnapped or forcibly brought here, it was enough to shut down Lost Lamb and put Francine out of business.

This wasn't the first incident during his time on the task force that Brady had been able to close down part of the human trafficking operation, but he was done playing Whack-a-Mole. He wanted more. He wanted to identify the people who were running this scheme and destroy their whole operation.

Francine glared at her charges. "Get back in the house."

"But we love the horses."

"It's dangerous for you to be here."

Grumbling, the two of them waddled out the barn door. The woman who had been reported missing turned her face up toward the sun and smiled. She didn't seem to be under any kind of restraint. If she'd wanted to escape, she could.

This missing woman had chosen to be here, and he couldn't blame her. Lost Lamb Ranch offered fresh air, food and shelter. She could even hang out in the barn with the horses. But this was a short-term solution. In exchange for this brief security, she was giving away her future and her freedom.

Brady had to close this place down before anyone else was lost.

TWO HOURS LATER, MARGARET drove Brady back to his house. Earlier, she'd introduced him to her three-year-old son, Jeremy—a quiet, sweet-faced kid who looked a lot like his mother. He'd make a good subject for a portrait, and Brady said he'd do it for free. It was a damn good thing that he wasn't trying to make a living as an artist.

During the brief drive, Margaret offered her friendship and a lot more. Talking to her was like walking a tightrope, trying not to reject and not to encourage at the same time.

He was glad to be home, especially when he walked through the front door and Petra came charging down the stairs with the fake wedding photo in her hands. She held it in front of her chest. "This is really good."

"Photoshop," he said.

"I remember this picture. I was at the beach, looking out at the waves. Now, I'm looking adoringly at you."

"Lucky for me, you were wearing a white muslin dress. Not exactly a standard wedding gown."

"But perfect for me." She placed the photo on the mantel and turned back to face him. "You're very talented. Why didn't you mention that you were the one who did the artwork?"

He didn't consider himself to be an artist. His portraits were a hobby, something he did to relax. "I meant to show you this morning, but we got rushed out the door too fast."

"You showed Margaret first."

"Jealous?"

"Hardly," she said. "But it came as a shock when I figured out that you were the painter. I might have blown our cover."

Even though he was anxious to hear what she'd learned from Dee and to start making plans, he couldn't resist taking a couple of minutes to tease. "Say what you want, but I know the truth. You're possessive about me."

She scoffed. "Am not."

"You don't want other women talking to me."

"Because I'm afraid they'll be squashed when you roll out your gigantic ego."

"You're cute when you're jealous."

Her blue eyes narrowed to slits. "Keep it up, smart guy. You know I'll get even."

"I'm done." He threw up his hands.

"That's good, because we need to take action. Lost Lamb needs to be shut down as soon as possible."

"I agree." Did she know something he didn't? "Why do you think so?"

"Dee is going to have her baby very soon, and I can't bear the thought of having that infant swept into an uncertain future. When she told me she was a surrogate, I thought maybe the baby would be all right, but then—"

"A surrogate?" This was a twist he hadn't heard before. "Are you sure?"

"Dr. Smith confirmed it. By the way, I should tell you that I'm all in favor of surrogacy. It's a good solution for a lot of couples trying to have a baby."

"I'm guessing that those aren't the couples who got involved with Lost Lamb."

"In most states, it's not illegal," she said. "The parents of a surrogate baby have the same rights as biological mothers and fathers. They don't have to take a test to prove they'll be good parents."

"Maybe they should." He thought of his own abusive father. "The world might be a better place if all parents were required to show they were worthy of the job."

"Dee is being paid, and she seems to be happy with the arrangement. Why is Lost Lamb using surrogates?"

"It's a big bucks business. And it dovetails neatly with human trafficking. Don't forget that these pregnant women and their babies are nothing more than human chattel to these people. After the mothers are used up as breeders, they might be forced into prostitution. Their children might suffer the same fate or be used for kid porn."

A shudder went through her. "It's hard to believe that can happen in this country."

"Cruelty is international. It's everywhere."

The crimes he'd witnessed while working on the human trafficking task force defied human decency, especially the horrors perpetrated against children who were forced into servitude, trained as mercenaries or raised to do whatever their minders demanded. It had to be stopped. He and Petra were the spearhead for law enforcement. If they could pierce the veil of secrecy surrounding the bosses, they might make a difference.

And they needed to get started. Much had happened since they left the house this morning and went their separate ways. He didn't want their information to be jumbled together in a rambling, emotional conversation. They needed a coherent sense of direction.

He went into the kitchen, flipped open his portfolio and took out a sketchpad. "We're going to sit at the table, have coffee and debrief. Then we'll come up with a plan of action."

"Coffee is necessary?"

"Absolutely."

She went to the counter to prepare a fresh pot. "Figure out all the plans you want."

He opened the sketchbook on the table in front of him and wrote the number *1*.

Chapter Thirteen

"I want to talk about Dee first," Petra said. "Can we put her name under number one?"

"She's not our top priority."

"For me, her baby is the most important thing."

"There's a broader goal," Brady reminded her.

Petra wasn't big on planning; she usually went with her feelings. Right now, her heart was telling her to save Dee's unborn child. As she measured grounds into the basket filter of the coffeemaker, she tried to explain. "I understand what you're saying. If we arrest the bosses, we can shut down the entire operation. But if—"

"Arrest the top guys, and we rescue dozens of babies and their mothers and all the others who are funneled through the human traffic pipeline."

She turned the coffeemaker on, went to the kitchen table and sat across from him. "Obviously, that's the greater good."

He leaned forward to study her. Absent-mindedly, he rubbed his fingers against the stubble that outlined his firm jaw. "You don't like my reasoning."

"If going after the bosses means that we stay undercover and watch while Dee's baby is taken, I can't do it. I can't sacrifice one, even if it means saving many others."

His gray eyes shone with empathy. "We'll have to do both."

"There's not much time. Dee could go into labor at any given moment."

"Moving fast requires efficiency and organization. Yes?"

She nodded. "We're on the same page."

He gave her hand a squeeze, and then he wrote "Dee" on the sketchpad. Under the name, he wrote "surrogate," then he asked, "What else?"

"She was recruited into the surrogate program and is being paid for her services." Petra remembered their conversation. "For the in vitro process, they used Dee's eggs. She's healthy and attractive, which makes her a good donor."

"Did Dr. Smith do the in vitro?"

"I didn't ask."

"Where was it done?"

"I don't know." Disappointed in herself, she frowned. "I guess I didn't do a very good job of interrogating Dee."

"You established trust," he said. "That's a necessary step before you dig for more information.

If she thinks you're her friend, she's more likely to tell the truth."

"Dee's quite the little liar. She faked having her water break and pretended to be in labor so Margaret would quit bugging her."

"Would you say she's childish?"

"Very."

"Easily manipulated?"

"Yes." She watched him make notes on the sketchpad. "Why are you asking these questions?"

"I want to determine if Dee will follow our instructions. Easily manipulated means we can't trust her, can't tell her that we're undercover. But do you think you can convince her to do what you say?"

"If it means getting what she wants, she'll do it. She's self-centered and needy." Petra pointed to the sketchpad. "Here's another observation. Robert is kind of in love with Dee."

Brady made a note. "Robert isn't a bad guy. He's loyal to Francine because that's his job, but if he saw Dee or any of the other girls being threatened, he might take our side."

The need for action pulsed through her. She'd been marking time for two hours while he did his sitting with Francine, and she needed to be active. Rising from the table, she paced around the counter and back again.

The aroma of brewed coffee wafted through the

kitchen. Caffeine probably wasn't a good idea. Not for her. She already had enough nervous energy to run a marathon. "How is this information helping us plan?"

"We need to have an idea how these people will react in a confrontation. Here's an example. If Robert is ordered to come after us, we need to remind him of Dee and the other girls who need his protection."

"Got it." Even though the coffee wasn't done, she pulled out the pot and filled a mug for him. "I think we can assume that dear little Margaret will do anything you say, but she'd love to throw me under the bus."

He wrote Margaret's name. "Her son is another source of motivation for her. She'll protect him."

"And the other people at Lost Lamb?"

"A couple of cowboys, they're henchmen for Francine. Not including Dee, I've seen five pregnant women." On the sketchpad, he wrote a note about missing persons. "One of them matched the photo of the woman who disappeared off the street in Denver."

Petra was shocked. "Is she all right?"

"She's not being held against her will. In fact, she looked content."

"How can that be?"

He took a sip of the coffee. "I didn't think of this until you mentioned that Dee was recruited as a surrogate. We assumed that the missing woman was forcibly grabbed, but she might have come along willingly. Somebody might have convinced her that Lost Lamb was the answer to all her problems."

"Interesting theory," she said. "And you figured that out from the information I got from Dee?"

"Right."

"So my talk with her was useful after all."

"We're partners," he said. "That's how it works."

She liked being his partner and his undercover wife. That fake wedding photo surprised her, mostly because they looked so natural together. When she'd first met Brady, she would have guessed that they had nothing in common. He had seemed like the kind of guy that her law-and-order family would adore. Brady fit her father's description of a good man—a man worthy of his daughter. Usually, that was enough to make her run in the opposite direction. Not that there was anything wrong with the men her father chose for her…except, possibly, that they might bore her into a coma.

But Brady wasn't like that. He was artistic, creative and open-minded. He actually had a sense of humor.

On his sketchpad, he wrote "Dr. Smith."

"Yes," she said, "he's very suspicious."

"Your impressions?"

"He has the bedside manner of a mortician. When he came into the birthing suite, he barely looked at Dee, and he made it clear that he thought women in labor were a nuisance."

"How did he feel about having you work at Lost Lamb?"

"He likes the idea of having a midwife so he won't be bothered with delivering babies. Do you think he's one of the bosses?"

"We'll soon find out." Brady raised his coffee cup to his lips and took another sip. "I planted a GPS tracking device on his SUV. I traced him as far as Durango, but I had to leave for my appointment with Francine."

"I wondered how long it would take you to start acting like a fed."

"Hey, you have your smudge sticks. I have my surveillance technology."

"And I like that about you." Finally, they had something more to do than sit around and wait. "Why are we sitting here? We should be following his route."

"Patience," he said. "We'll go after nightfall when we won't be so obvious."

In capital letters, he wrote Francine's name on the sketchpad. Petra immediately pictured the stern, black-haired woman with the Cleopatra eyes. This was her opportunity to get back at Brady for his earlier teasing. "Ah, yes. You and

Francine. Tell me, Picasso, did she want to pose in the nude?"

"She wanted something with a horse, but I talked her out of it. This is going to be a tame portrait except for the cleavage and the riding crop."

He frowned into his coffee mug. His uneasiness was evident, and she noticed that he'd underlined Francine. The pressure he used to write her name made the printing darker than his other notes. "You think she's important."

"Maybe." He looked down at his sketchbook as though he hoped to see the words coalesce into an answer. "Francine is in charge at Lost Lamb, but I'm not sure where she fits into the overall operation. Over ninety percent of the traffickers I've come into contact with are men, and they're vicious. I don't see these guys taking orders from a woman."

"Sexism aside, Francine isn't a typical lady. She's tough and has a prison record."

"She served less than two years for various charges related to the time when she was a madam."

Petra pointed out, "Running a house of prostitution is a form of trafficking."

"It's not the same." He leaned back in the kitchen chair and stretched his long legs out straight in front of him. "About three months ago, we picked up a guy in San Diego who was transporting women overseas as sex slaves. He lived in a mansion in the hills with marble floors and three swimming pools. Gold was his trademark. He wore gold earrings. His four front teeth were solid gold."

"Charming," she said.

"While we were holding him in jail, he gouged out the eyes of the man in the cell next to him. He said that's what would happen to anyone who testified against him. Those witnesses would be blinded."

"Did you make the charges stick?"

"We got him on racketeering charges for bringing aliens into the country, kidnapping and extortion. He's in solitary in a super-max penitentiary." Brady slowly sipped his coffee. "How do you think Francine would handle a man like that?"

"A person like that…" A trickle of fear oozed down her spine. If Brady had meant to remind her that they were dealing with dangerous people, he'd succeeded. "A person like that can't be controlled by anyone or anything. He's like an inferno, unstoppable until he burns himself out. Who turned him in?"

"There were no witnesses. We picked up one of his trucks and traced the ownership. Once he was on our radar, evidence wasn't hard to compile."

"I'm guessing he had a front, some kind of legitimate business."

"You see things like a cop." His voice held a note of surprise. "I keep forgetting your background. Yeah, he had businesses. A couple of nightclubs."

"Francine has Lost Lamb." Petra reached forward and traced the letters on the sketchpad with the tip of her finger. "You wrote her name bigger and heavier than anything else on the page. Whether you have evidence, your intuition is telling you that she's important."

"Intuition?"

"What would you call it? Gut reaction?"

"Let's go with subconscious response. That makes you right and lets me think I'm still being rational."

She grinned. "You're cute when you compromise."

He stood and picked up his sketchpad. "How about if we see what Francine has to say for herself. I planted a bug in her office."

BRADY'S ART STUDIO ON the second floor fascinated Petra. While she was alone at the house and he was at Lost Lamb, she'd crept inside like a trespasser, even though he hadn't told her that his space was off-limits. As she explored, she'd become more comfortable, much the way she'd been with Brady himself. His studio was a reflection of the man.

His organization was spectacular. All the supplies and artworks were arranged in a neat, precise manner. Drop cloths covered the hardwood floor under the easel. Boxes with pencils and charcoal lined the space beside the drafting table. Acrylic paints were grouped by colors. His paintbrushes were in containers, ranging in size from a tiny swab to a three-inch-wide brush. She had no doubt that he knew the exact location of each and every item.

Contrasting this neatness were the portraits with their intense sensitivity and wild, unfettered creativity. In his sketches and paintings, he used a wide variety of subjects—men and women, young and old, beautiful and grotesque. There was a man with a weak chin, an easy smile and dark, scary eyes. Brady had drawn him repeatedly, always emphasizing the eyes.

Brady escorted her into his studio. "I assume you've looked around because you found the fake wedding photo."

She drew up short. "Should I have asked permission?"

"Not at all. I don't keep secrets from my fake wife." He crossed to the high stool in front of the drafting table. "Any questions?"

She went to the bin where the sketches of the man with scary eyes were kept and pulled one out. "I'm guessing this is someone you arrested."

"I wasn't the arresting agent, but I interviewed him a half dozen times. He'd be a nice guy if he wasn't a serial killer."

"I knew there was something crazy about him."

"Sick," he said, "not crazy."

She went to a painting of a woman with gray eyes and a high forehead who was thoughtfully arranging flowers. "This has to be your twin sister."

"You're right. That's Barbara."

Petra couldn't say why or what technique he'd used, but the painting radiated warmth and love. "It's obvious how much you care about her."

"You've got to love a twin. If you don't, it's like hating yourself."

He turned to his drafting table. The wooden top was hinged so it could be raised to an angle when he was sketching. He lifted the top and completely removed it. Inside was a flat surface—a drawer about four inches deep where he kept his surveillance electronics. In the back corner, she spotted his Beretta.

"Very slick," she said.

"You didn't notice it was here?"

"No, but I wasn't looking."

Underneath the table was another compartment. He reached down and took out another automatic handgun. "It's loaded and ready to go. There's another ammo clip behind it."

There was only one reason he'd be showing her the weapons. "Do you expect to be attacked here at the house?"

"I want to be prepared for anything." He returned the gun to the cache. Reaching inside the desk, he flipped the switch on a rectangular black box with four dials. "This is the receiver for the bug I planted in Francine's office. The dials are for volume. That bug is number one. I have capability for four."

He turned up the volume. There was the sound of shuffling papers but no voices.

She asked, "Does it only play in real time?"

"There's a six-hour loop which is automatically downloaded. Push the reverse button and it plays back from the start of the six hours."

She peered over his shoulder. "And this is fast forward."

"Let's back it up and find out if Francine said anything about my session with her."

He manipulated the transmitter to play back a conversation that took place less than an hour ago. Apparently, Francine was on the phone, and they only heard her side.

"About this midwife," she said. "If she does well with Dee, I might put her on retainer. Smith agrees. He's tired of wasting his time with these pregnant women."

There was a pause while she listened.

Then she said, "I have no reason to trust her other than she's motivated by money. You should have seen the look on her face when her husband offered to paint my portrait for free."

Brady shot her a glance. "You didn't approve?"

"You were selling yourself short."

Francine continued, "If she demands too much I won't use her. That's simple enough. Even you ought to be able to understand that."

She paused again to listen. When she spoke, her tone was curt. "I'm not taking a risk. There's no reason for the midwife to be suspicious. She won't see any of your paperwork. Smith can still sign the birth certificates."

Another pause.

"I know you're just doing your job," Francine said, "a job I pay you very well to do. May I remind you that there are plenty of other lawyers I could hire?"

Petra squeezed Brady's arm and whispered the name of the lawyer in Durango. "Stan Mancuso."

"Fine," Francine said. "You can stop by tomorrow at ten. If the midwife and her husband prove to be a problem, we can always arrange for an accident."

Chapter Fourteen

Francine's threat echoed through Brady's mind. From the start, he'd known that their undercover operation had an element of danger, but actually hearing the threat brought the message home to him. They could be hurt. He wanted Petra out of there.

"An accident?" She scoffed. "As if I'd stand back and let that happen."

"We have to take Francine seriously."

"You bet we do. She was talking to that lawyer as if she was his boss. Tomorrow, when we listen in on her chat with Mancuso, we're going to find out a lot."

In her clear blue eyes, he saw anger and determination. Not a trace of fear. "It might be time to pull the plug."

"You're kidding, right?"

"This isn't your job, Petra. You're not an agent. I have no right to put you in harm's way."

"It's my decision, and I'm not ready to back down."

"Your safety is my number one responsibility." It had taken some fast talking on his part to get approval to use a civilian on this undercover operation. "If this assignment goes haywire, it's my judgment that will be called into question."

"Are you telling me that you want to end this project because of your reputation?"

"My career is…important to me."

"More important than Dee's baby?"

As he looked down at the surveillance electronics he'd hidden in the drafting table, he exhaled a weary sigh. His life had been easier before he met this woman. Before Petra, his objective had been clear—promotion to the Behavioral Analysis Unit. Each step he took was designed to lead him closer to that goal.

Knowing her had changed his focus. He couldn't lie to himself, couldn't pretend that he was concerned about her for purely professional reasons. Francine's threat scared the hell out of him. He couldn't allow Petra to leap into danger without considering the consequences. He cared about her, cared more deeply than he wanted to acknowledge.

"I can't put you in danger," he said.

"Don't treat me like I'm helpless." She turned her back on him, paced to the door and came back at him. "You saw my scores from the training at Quantico. I'm expert at hand-to-hand combat."

"That was a long time ago," he reminded her.

"I'm also a very good markswoman."

He liked her spirit but hated that she was so stubborn. "When was the last time you fired a gun?"

"A couple of months ago," she said. "I did some target practice and I was—"

"Wait." He needed to put an end to this discussion. "When was the last time you fired a gun at a human being?"

She swallowed hard. "Never."

"Your job is to bring life into the world. Not the opposite." He reached toward her, but she backed away. His hand fell loosely to his side. "I can't take the risk that something bad might happen to you."

She pivoted on her heel and left his studio. He was glad that she'd accepted his decision, even though it meant they wouldn't be spending any more time together. Her safety came first.

He pulled down the lid on his drafting table. Logically, he knew there was evidence to be found using the GPS tracking on Smith's vehicle and listening on the bug to Francine's conversations. But it would have to be handled in another way. This undercover assignment was over.

There had been those on the task force who

had told him this wouldn't work. They'd advised against using a private citizen who wasn't an agent, and they'd been correct. He'd made a mistake, not that his career mattered as much as the possible danger to Petra. There had been special moments between them, laughing together and teasing. When they'd kissed almost by accident, he had hoped there might be something more.

A false hope. He should have known that he'd never have a chance with a spontaneous woman like her. She was a free spirit, a butterfly that was meant to be admired and never caged by the rules and cautions he lived by.

She called to him, "I need to show you something."

He left the studio and went into her bedroom. Standing beside her neatly made bed, she held up a framed photograph. "I want you to take a good, hard look at this picture," she said. "It's my family. That's my dad in his fire inspector uniform, my brother the cop and my sister in her Army fatigues. Me and Mom are wearing our SFPD T-shirts."

They were a good-looking family—the type of people he wished he'd grown up with. "Your brother has red hair like you."

"It's really more of a blond, but that's not the point," she said. "I was brought up understanding what it meant to serve and protect. In my family, those aren't just lofty ideals. It's how we live. We take care of people who need help. I wanted to be an FBI agent so I could make a difference."

"But you quit."

"For personal reasons," she said, "but I never stopped wanting to help people or to fight for those who can't take care of themselves. That's in my blood. I can't imagine a worse crime than human trafficking. I don't want to be scared off."

He could see the passion crackling through her, lighting her eyes and turning her cheeks rosy. She was on fire. When she dragged her fingers through her hair, pushing wisps back into her ponytail, he expected to see sparks flying around her.

"This isn't about being scared," he said. "It's about caution."

"Let me ask you a question, Brady. Why did you ask me to do this in the first place?"

"As a midwife, you'd have a natural way to get inside Lost Lamb."

"That, my friend, was a good bit of strategy. Look how well it worked."

He was still thinking of Francine's casual mention of an "accident" that might befall those who got in her way. "A death threat? You consider that a step in the right direction?"

"Francine also said that she wants to put me on

retainer. She likes my grabby money-comes-first attitude. Even Dr. Smith approves of me."

"True."

"In a matter of hours, Patty and Brady Gilliam have gotten closer to these people than anybody else could. We need to play this out." She tossed the photograph on the bed and took a step closer to him. "Trust me. When we close down this human trafficking ring, your career will be golden."

She stood so close that he could smell the wildflower fragrance that radiated from her. No human being should smell so good. She amazed him on so many levels. Her nearness eclipsed his logic. All he wanted was to gather her into his arms, hold her and kiss her sweet, soft lips. "I don't care about my promotion."

"But you said—"

"I know what I said." He reached toward her and lightly stroked her upper arm. "During the time we've been together, I haven't thought about my career. I hadn't realized it until just now, but I haven't been visualizing that name plate on my desk at the BAU in Quantico."

"Why not?"

"There isn't room in my head to think of anything but you."

Surprise registered in her gaze, but she didn't

back away from him. "Are you feeding me a line?"

"Like trying to pick you up by asking you to come home with me and see my sketches?"

"Exactly like that." The hint of a smile softened her determined expression.

His hand molded her shoulder. He exerted a subtle pressure, drawing her closer. "Showing you my sketches isn't a line because I really am an artist. Wanting to be with you isn't a line, either."

"Why?"

"Because I'm a man."

Only a few inches separated them, and she closed the gap. The tips of her breasts grazed his chest. Her arms reached around his neck. When she went up on tiptoe and kissed him, a rush of pure sensation chased through his blood. He couldn't think. There was no logic.

He closed his arms around her, holding her tightly, melding their bodies together. He wanted to be one with her, to make love to this incredible, beautiful, sensual woman. He could feel her breath join with his. As she adjusted her embrace, her body rubbed against him, setting off a chain reaction that was more arousing than he could have ever anticipated.

Unable to hold back, he deepened their kiss. His tongue penetrated her mouth, claiming her. She responded with searing passion. They were generating enough fire to melt steel, but there wasn't anything hard about her. Her slender curves were firm and toned and one-hundred-percent perfect.

He caressed her, memorizing the dip of her waist and the flare of her hips. When he felt her pulling away, he didn't want to let her go. This kiss should last for an eternity.

She leaned away from him, gasping. "Wow," she whispered.

"Been thinking," he said. "If we're going to pull off our undercover identities as a married couple, we should be sleeping in the same bed."

He swept her off her feet and carried her into his bedroom. Gently, he stretched her out on his bedspread. As she lay back, she unfastened her ponytail. Her thick, auburn hair fanned out on the pillow. She was flushed. Her eyes dilated. She was ready to make love.

When he leaned down to kiss her, she raised her hand. "Wait."

Confused, he studied her. He hadn't read the signals wrong. She wanted to make love as much as he did. "Why?"

"It's not that I don't want to make love to you because I do. I really do." Her voice was husky. "But I know you're a serious guy—not the kind of man who has casual flings."

She didn't understand men as well as she thought. Most guys—himself included—had indulged in an occasional one-night stand. He wasn't about to start listing the women he'd slept with. Not that it was a long roll call. But he sure as hell wasn't a saint. "You're right about one thing. I want more than a fling with you."

"There's something I need to tell you."

Unless she was about to confess to being an ax murderer, he couldn't imagine anything that would dampen his desire for her. "Go ahead."

She wriggled across the bedspread until she was sitting with her back to the headboard and her knees pulled up. To him, it looked like a defensive position, as though she wanted to protect herself from him or from the way she was feeling. Whatever was holding her back was important; he had to take her seriously.

"I know," she said, "that I come across as a free spirit, but I'm really kind of traditional. I've had only two other relationships in my life that were important to me. They both ended badly."

Although his heart was beating so hard that it felt like it was going to crash through his rib cage, he reined in his desire. "You told me about the cop who was shot, the guy you left your training at Quantico for."

"Who then dumped me," she said.

"Tell me about the other one."

"I was in college. We were going to get married."

Petra lowered her head and closed her eyes.

In her mind, she flashed back to that painful time. She'd finished up her degree at Berkeley and had moved in with her long-time lover. Marriage had been somewhere on their horizon, but neither of them were in a rush.

Looking back, she could see that she'd been in a rebellious phase, even though she'd never intended to thwart her family's values. She'd wanted to make her own way, to blaze her own trails. And then, she'd gotten pregnant.

The timing hadn't been stellar, but it wasn't as though she'd planned for this to happen. She still remembered when she took the early pregnancy test and confirmed that she was going to have a baby. An unexpected joy had surged through her. She'd felt alive, really alive.

Her boyfriend hadn't been equally thrilled. He'd wanted adventure and excitement which he hadn't been able to imagine with children. A rift had separated them. She'd been torn between her love for him and her love for the unborn child growing within her. Three weeks later, she'd made a decision. She'd chosen the baby, no matter what the consequence for the relationship.

He'd walked out. Two days later, she'd started bleeding. Her doctor had diagnosed an ectopic pregnancy with the fetus growing in the fallopian tube. Her baby hadn't been viable. Her miscarriage had led to laparoscopic surgery, scarring and a strong probability that she would never be able to have children. It wasn't impossible for her to conceive, but she knew that the odds weighed heavily against her.

"Petra, are you all right?"

She looked into Brady's concerned eyes. He was a good man. Before he got too deeply involved with her, he deserved to know that she couldn't provide him with children.

"I was just remembering," she said.

"Your college lover?"

"The relationship ended over a difference in lifestyles. He wanted to be a selfish pig, and I didn't."

"It changed you."

"Oh, yeah." The scars were more than physical. The miscarriage caused her to rethink her somewhat aimless drifting through life. "That's when I decided to become an FBI agent."

"As opposed to a selfish pig?"

"I told you before, I want to help people. Law enforcement seemed to be the family business, except for Mom."

"And your Greek grandmother," he said.

She remembered the story she'd told him about her yaya. "You psychology types are really sneaky. I've never talked so much about myself."

"I'm still listening."

She couldn't believe she was in bed with this sexy, gorgeous man and not making love to him. He kissed the way he did everything else—with incredible skill. When he'd lifted her off her feet and carried her to his bed, she felt like she was literally being swept away. "I don't want you to be my therapist."

"And I didn't apply for the job."

His gaze was warm, even hot. If she reached for him, she knew they'd be ripping off their clothes and making love. And she wanted to have sex with him.

Now wasn't the time. Not yet. "I think it's better if we concentrate on something else. Weren't we going to follow the GPS tracking on Dr. Smith?"

"Really?" His gaze was incredulous. "Now, you want to talk about investigating. Right now?"

What she really wanted was to erase the mistakes she'd made in the past. The best she could hope for was to make the future better. "Let's get started."

Chapter Fifteen

In spite of Petra's insistence that they get down to serious investigating right away, Brady was determined to wait until after dark to follow the GPS trail left by Dr. Smith. Continuing their undercover assignment in the face of a stated threat went against his better judgment, and he'd be damned if he let himself be pushed into any disorganized action that he deemed dangerous. From now on, there would be no leaping without making sure they had a safe landing.

Pacing in the studio, he outlined his position. "We need to coordinate all our actions. Above all, exercise caution."

"I get it," she said. "My new mantra is No Risk."

"Good."

"What if Dee goes into labor?"

"When we get to that bridge…"

"…we'll cross it," she said brightly.

"In the meantime, we plan."

"And I'll carry a couple of extra crystals. Amethyst and obsidian are good for protection."

"Oh, swell."

He wondered if she had anything in her bag of tricks that would alleviate the intense, unreasonable desire he felt for her. He could barely glance in her direction without becoming aroused, and passion was the opposite of what was needed. His natural inclination on the job was to be cool, detached and controlled, but their kiss and the promise of making love tapped into a different part of his psyche.

Even though he wasn't a Freudian, his current state reminded him of Sigmund's theory of the id—a part of the human mind where instinct and libido ran rampant. Brady had a clear mental picture of his own id as a hairy-toed, slobbering, grunting beast that bounced off the walls and rolled across the floor, demanding attention. The id had a mantra of its own: me want woman. But Petra didn't want to play.

Exerting the full force of discipline he'd developed over the years, Brady turned to the task at hand. He played back the recording of Francine's conversation with the Durango lawyer. A couple of questions arose.

"She mentioned birth certificates," he said. "Is that usually your responsibility?"

"Frequently, but not always. The Certificate of Live Birth needs to be signed and registered with the state."

"What happens if it's not registered?"

"I don't think anything happens until the child actually needs a birth certificate for identification or enrolling in school."

With his id firmly tied down, he regained his sense of logic. "If the birth isn't reported, the state doesn't know the child exists. The baby can't be considered missing because it was never there in the first place. These babies would be untraceable."

"What's the advantage in that?"

"They have no identity until one is assigned to them. These children could be raised for slave labor or as mercenaries."

"Is that efficient?" she questioned. "Raising a child is expensive."

"If it's done right," he said grimly. "These children wouldn't be properly cared for. They'd be human strays. We need to get a look at that lawyer's paperwork."

"Is it on computer?" she asked.

"The FBI tech team already hacked into Stan Mancuso's system. They didn't find anything to send up red flags. Investigating him is going to require a field trip to Durango."

But if he and Petra showed up on Mancuso's doorstep, their cover was blown. He wanted to maintain their access at Lost Lamb for as long as possible. Petra had been correct when she said

Francine sounded like the boss in her conversation with Mancuso. That woman with the black wigs and the Cleopatra eyes was a lot more dangerous than he'd expected.

Fortunately, he wasn't on his own. Brady had access to backup in the person of Cole McClure, a legendary undercover agent.

He paused in his pacing to face Petra. Immediately, his libidinous id started gurgling and flailing. But Brady kept his voice calm and even. "I'm going to put in a call to Cole. After that, we're going to do a drill for what to do if we're attacked at the house."

She bobbed her head in a reasonable facsimile of cooperation. "I'll go downstairs and make tea. Do you want more coffee?"

"Sounds good, thanks."

As he watched her leave the studio, it took all his willpower not to give in to the beast id and make a grab for her. Maybe there was time for a cold shower before she came back upstairs.

WHEN PETRA RETURNED to the studio carrying her herbal tea and Brady's coffee, he was still on the phone with Cole. Standing in front of his easel, Brady had his back to her as he drew on a sheet of white paper tacked to a paint-stained board. He gestured emphatically with his charcoal pencil, making a point with Cole and then returning to his sketch. It was a rough portrait of her face.

Fascinated, she watched as her features became clearer. Was her mouth that big? Was her chin really that pointy? She'd never been someone who spent a lot of time looking in mirrors. Her makeup regime was minimal, and her hair required little care beyond washing and letting it air dry. Brady made her look interesting—not Barbie doll pretty but somehow striking, with high, strong cheekbones. She'd always been too distracted by her freckles to pay attention to her cheekbones.

The shadings of his pencil gave her features depth and added texture to her hair. Her closed-mouth smile was subtle with a quirk at the corners, as though she knew a secret that she wasn't telling. With a few artistic strokes, he made her eyes light up. As with all of his portraits, she perceived an emotional undertone. The face that stared from his sketch—her face—was sensual and lively.

He finished his phone call and the sketch at the same time. Without turning around, he asked, "Do you like it?"

"I look like somebody who's ready for a challenge." *In the bedroom maybe.* "I like it a lot."

When he turned and came toward her, he seemed more calm and in control. He took the steaming coffee mug from her and lifted it to his mouth. As he sipped, he gazed at her over the brim. His voice was low, just a shade above a whisper. "You're a good subject."

"Is that another one of your lines?"

"Do I need one?"

Not really. When she looked into the faceted gray of his eyes, she was mesmerized—anxious to fall into his arms and not really sure why she was holding back. *Oh, yeah, because she was terrified.* She was afraid to tell him her deepest secrets. It was probably for the best. He wasn't planning to stay in Colorado, anyway.

She asked, "What did Cole say?"

"He'll go to Durango tomorrow. While Mancuso has his appointment with Francine, Cole will be undercover at his offices."

"One less problem we have to deal with."

He nodded. "Now, for the safety drill."

"Do we really have to do this? I know what to do if somebody attacks me."

"Fine," he said, "you tell me. Somebody busts in the door or sneaks upstairs while you're sleeping, what do you do?"

Her training on surprise attacks came not only from sessions at Quantico. Her brother and sister liked to play commando. They were always hiding and jumping out at each other and at her.

"The first objective is escape," she said. "If somebody comes after us at the house, they won't be alone and they won't be gentle. I won't engage in combat unless there's no other alternative."

"Good answer," he said. "Suppose you're upstairs, how do you make your exit?"

"Easy." Mug in hand, she left the studio. As soon as she walked through his bedroom door, her gaze went to the bedspread which was still messy from where they'd been lying together. Sensuality hung in the air; she could almost smell the pheromones.

She opened a door with a glass window that led onto the balcony that stretched across the front of the house. The cedar flooring was about five-feet deep and there were a couple of lawn chairs shoved up against the wall of the house. The balcony faced west and would be a perfect place for sunning in the afternoon.

Turning to him, she said, "I'd climb over the railing and drop to the ground."

"What if the attacker is watching the front of the house?"

"I'd have to open one of the windows in the studio and pull the same maneuver. A longer drop but still doable." She frowned. "In this scenario, where are you?"

"Gone."

"What's that supposed to mean? Gone?" *As in dead?* She didn't want to participate in an exercise where they were pretending the worst had happened. "No negative energy. I'm going to imagine you've gone out to get a cappuccino. This is my cappuccino defense."

"Whatever."

He moved to the railing where he stood watching the colors of sunset paint the skies above the treetops. A breeze blew his hair back from his high, intelligent forehead, and sunlight burnished his face and shoulders. He looked almost too good to be true. Sipping her tea, she kept her hands busy so she wouldn't be tempted to touch him.

"I wish," she said, "I wish we had more time."

"We're cramming a lot of action into just a few hours. That's for damn sure."

"Your accent just got heavy. When you said 'for damn sure,' you really sounded like Texas."

"It's where I'm from." He shrugged. "My grandpa used to say that you can change where you're going, but you can't change where you've been."

There was a lot of truth in those homespun sayings. She could never erase her past; those scars were permanent. But a future relationship with Brady could lead in directions she hadn't even imagined.

Leaning against the railing beside him, she asked, "Did I pass the test for escaping an attack?"

"I suppose." He grinned at her and his dimple

appeared. "Let me show you the weapons I've got hidden around and about."

"More guns?"

"The only firearms are in the studio, but there are plenty of other ways to defend yourself."

He took her on a tour, and she was surprised to discover that virtually every room held a concealed arsenal. In the bedrooms and bathroom upstairs, there were containers with innocuous labels that actually held pepper spray. Knives were tucked between the cushions of the chairs and sofa. Several blunt instruments—ranging from a hammer to a golf club—were placed strategically. No matter where she was in the house, she was only a few steps away from a potentially lethal weapon.

She looked up at him. "This is amazing."

"Planning ahead, it's what I do." He took out his car keys. "It's almost dark. Let's go follow Smith's GPS track."

"I'll be ready in a flash."

Rifling through the clothes in her closet, she tried to plan for what the rest of the evening might bring. They might be chasing bad guys, which meant she'd need a decent pair of shoes. And they might be sneaking around in the dark, so her outfit needed to be black. Quickly, she dressed in dark jeans and a black sweatshirt.

She was halfway down the stairs before she remembered another essential. They needed luck. She zipped back to her room and grabbed a necklace with an amethyst stone.

BRADY HAD PROGRAMMED the route taken by Dr. Smith into a handheld GPS device that gave precise directions. With Petra behind the wheel of the truck, he was free to visually scan as they drove through the unfamiliar territory. Not that he could see much beyond the beam of their headlights.

The ITEP task force had already pinpointed this area—known as Four Corners because it was where Colorado, Utah, Arizona and New Mexico met—as a good distribution hub. From here, the human cargo could be shipped in a variety of directions that crossed borders and law enforcement jurisdictions. In addition to the four different states, the Navajo and Hopi Indian reservations were nearby.

No wonder the task force had spent months and uncovered very little. Even a small lead, like the tracker on Smith's car, represented forward progress. Brady hoped that he and Petra would uncover evidence that would lead to the top men. Or the top woman, he reminded himself. Francine couldn't be discounted.

As they drove through Kirkland, he pointed out the partly burned sign for Royal Burger. It read, Roya urge. "The food is okay but not exactly fit for a king. Are you hungry?"

"I could eat. We can grab something in Durango."

He liked that she wasn't picky about her food. Like him, Petra seemed to eat as an afterthought in spite of her childhood experiences in the kitchen of a Greek restaurant. "Do you know how to make baklava?"

"Of course." She shot him a questioning glance. "Where did that question come from?"

"Just getting to know you."

"Do you have a cooking specialty?"

"I'm from Texas, lady. My three-alarm barbecue can't be beat. Even my twin admits that mine is the best."

"Your twin," she said, "I'd like to meet her."

As a general rule, Brady avoided bringing women to meet his sister. Barbara was so anxious for him to settle down that she tended to pounce. "If I brought you two ladies together, you'd conspire to drive me crazy. I'd have to go hide in the doghouse with my four-year-old nephew."

"A good place for you," she teased. "Needless to say, my father would love you."

He flopped back in the passenger seat as if he'd been punched in the chest. "That's the kiss of death."

"What do you mean?"

"In my experience, women aren't interested in being with men their fathers approve of."

"You sound like this has happened to you before." She chuckled. "Well, of course it has. Not only are you a clean, decent guy but you're special agent. And you know how to fix cars. Dads have got to love you."

"And that's not what their daughters are looking for."

"I've already done my rebellious phase," she said. "I'd be happy for my dad to like you."

He watched her as she drove. Sketching her had calmed his crazy id-driven passion, and he was attracted in a different, more purposeful way. When he'd told her that he wanted more than a fling, he hadn't been lying. She was someone special. He hadn't been looking for a woman like her. With her yoga and crystals and positive energy, Petra didn't seem like she'd fit into his life. Somehow, she did. They meshed. He hadn't been looking, but he'd found her just the same.

In Durango, they drove the same route as Dr. Smith. It appeared that he was just taking care of errands, making stops at a hardware store and a grocery store. After they grabbed a couple of chicken sandwiches at a drive-through, they returned on the same road they drove into town.

About five miles from Kirkland, they exited onto a two-lane road into a pine forest. Studying the GPS map, Brady noted there were few turnoffs on the road. He considered getting out of the truck and walking closer to where Smith made his stop but decided to see where they were headed first.

"At the next fork in the road, go right. Smith stopped at one-point-three miles, but we're going to drive past." He remembered what happened when he attempted the same maneuver at the Lost Lamb. "No stopping. I doubt Smith would recognize our truck, but it's better if we're not seen."

"Got it," she said.

"Tell me when we've gone a mile."

She nodded and sat up a little straighter behind the steering wheel. A sweeping curve in the road led to a more rugged area where the trees blended with jagged rock formations.

"It's a mile," she said. "One-point-one."

In the flash of their headlights, he saw the multilevel house with a deck that jutted into the forest like the prow of a boat. The modern architecture and redwood color seemed to grow organically from the forested surroundings. As they got closer, moonlight illuminated a very large house. Smith's SUV was parked in front.

It wasn't exactly clear what Dr. Smith did for the human trafficking organization, but he was obviously well-paid.

Chapter Sixteen

Dodging on foot through the moonlit forest, Petra was glad she'd taken the time to dress appropriately. Her sweatshirt protected her from low-hanging branches, and her hiking boots allowed her to move quickly, keeping pace with Brady's longer stride.

They'd parked the truck in the driveway of a vacant house that was about a mile and a half down the road from Smith's sprawling home. She'd gotten only a glimpse of the place as she drove past, but she was impressed.

Brady turned to check on her progress. Even though they were still quite a distance from Smith's house, he kept his voice low. "Are you doing all right?"

"Yoga isn't my only exercise. I jog a couple of miles, twice a week." Her heart was pumping harder than usual, but it wasn't because of the exercise. She was excited. Brady might go chasing after bad guys all the time, but she didn't. "What do you expect to find here?"

"I don't know. Hell, I don't even know for sure that this is Smith's house. The mailbox had numbers but no name."

"We don't even know for sure that Smith is his name. The first time he introduced himself, I almost laughed. Smith is such an obvious alias."

Brady leaned his back against a tree trunk. In his dark cargo pants and black jacket with his Beretta clipped to his hip, he looked like he could handle anything. "Finding this place is a break for us. There's a lot we can learn if we don't get caught."

"We won't." She pumped up her positive thinking to counteract his negative attitude. "We're going to get close to the house and observe. We will find evidence. Then, we'll go back to the truck."

He rubbed his hand across his T-shirt. "I should be wearing my bulletproof vest. And I should have brought one for you, too."

"When you're undercover, you can't be prepared for everything."

"Risky," he muttered.

"Stop it." She grabbed his arm and gave a little shake. "No negative vibes. This is going to turn out well. I promise you it will."

He ducked his head and gave her a light kiss on the cheek. "You're right."

The easy intimacy startled her, but she liked it. "We're going to get these guys."

Pushing away from the tree, he started climbing the incline at the side of the road, and she followed. The incline wasn't steep, but the sliver of a moon gave off very little light. The footing was difficult, and she stumbled more than once.

At the top of the ridge, Brady found a path that was wide enough to allow them to walk side by side. She hoped he knew where he was going. It was easy to get lost in the mountains in the dark.

Quietly, she said, "I had the impression that Smith hasn't been working at Lost Lamb for very long."

"Same here. Margaret said something about how things were easier now that they had a doctor."

"How is he affording this house? Francine is tight with the purse strings, and she wouldn't pay him a lot to deliver babies." She glanced at Brady. The moonlight slanted across his high forehead and strong jaw. "What do you think is going on?"

"Smith is more than a baby doc. His skill might have something to do with the surrogates." He turned toward the right. "We're close. It's this way."

"How can you tell?"

"My unfailing sense of direction," he said.

"You must have been a star in Boy Scouts."

He held up an electronic device. "Or it might be this handy-dandy GPS unit. I programmed the address in here."

She hadn't known that the GPS unit could give walking directions. His little gadget was probably a super-FBI version.

At the top of the hill, he paused and pointed. They were looking down at the multilevel, modern house. The top floor, closest to where they were standing, had one wall that was all windows— perfect for them to peek inside. Unfortunately, the room was dark. The only lights were on the middle floor where there were a lot of windows and a wide deck.

Brady hunkered down beside a chunky granite rock, and she sat beside him. Excitement rushed through her. This was a real investigation, the kind of thing she'd envisioned herself doing if she'd become an FBI agent. She wished that she had a gun, but Brady was already beating himself up because they didn't have his-and-hers bulletproof vests, so she decided not to mention the lack. "Should we get closer?"

"Not unless there's something to see."

That was logical and, at the same time, didn't make sense. "How do we know if—"

"Sit quietly and observe. We want to figure out how many people are in that house."

"Like guards?"

"It's possible, especially if the house belongs to one of the bosses. And it's likely that the area is protected by motion detectors or mini-cams."

"How can you tell?"

"If we move closer, I can spot the surveillance equipment, but we'll probably set off the alarms." He dug into one of the pockets in his cargo pants and took out a set of binoculars that he handed to her. "These are regular and night vision."

She held them up to her eyes. Using the infrared vision, she scanned the area. Details became clear. "I can see everything."

"That's the point."

"No guards."

"Keep looking." He sat on the ground beside her and draped his arm loosely around her shoulder. "They don't know we're here. We've got time."

Peering through the windows on the middle floor, she wasn't able to see anyone or anything unusual. There was no one outside. The landscaping and the architecture were, however, spectacular. Even the firewood was stacked artistically. Clear water bubbled through a fountain shaped like a pagoda in a rock garden.

After a while, she got tired of searching and not finding. She leaned back, fitting herself into a comfortable position against Brady's chest. Her ear pressed against his T-shirt and she listened to the strong, steady beat of his heart. The cool of the night contrasted the warmth of his body. She should have been relaxed and cozy, but she was too amped about being on what amounted to a stakeout.

His embrace felt so very wonderful. Only a few hours ago, she'd been in his bed. *And she'd turned him down.* Was she crazy? Maybe Brady wasn't meant for a long-term relationship with her, but there was no way she'd refuse to make love to him again.

His hand tightened on her arm. "Something's happening at the house."

The lights in the top level went on. Through the windows, they could see into what appeared to be a huge bedroom with an equally huge bed, a giant television and an exercise bike. Using the binoculars, she spotted Smith's bald, white head. "It's him. Alone."

Instead of a pristine lab coat, he was wearing shorts and a T-shirt. He climbed onto the stationary bike and used a remote to turn on the television news.

"What do you think?" she asked with a grin. "Should we call out the National Guard?"

"This is way too normal. He's not even watching cable."

"Even bad guys have their favorite news anchors."

"Back to the truck." He stood and held out a hand to help her up. "There's one other place that the GPS tracker showed him stopping. It's between here and Lost Lamb."

She bounced to her feet and handed the binoculars to him. "We certainly don't want to miss one thrill-packed minute of Dr. Smith's day."

"Welcome to the wonderful world of investigation," he said. "There's a lot of watching and waiting and being bored to death. Then, blam."

"Blam?"

"Like the night we met, when we found baby Miguel and his mother."

She remembered it well, especially the sight of him diving through the air, risking his life to save Miguel and his mom. "That was maybe too much excitement."

As they headed back toward the place where they'd left the truck, she kept her eyes down, watching her footing on the rugged terrain. Even though the night was quiet and the road was utterly deserted, she had the feeling that they weren't alone. She heard nothing but the wind through the tree branches. She saw no one else but felt a prickling between her shoulder blades as though someone was watching.

Descending the hillside, she slipped. Although

she caught herself before she went sprawling, she
went down on one knee. Facing the opposite hill,
she looked up and saw the distant silhouette of a
figure on horseback.

Brady stepped in front of her, cutting off her
vision. "Are you okay?"

"I'm fine."

When she looked around him, the horse was
gone. Nothing there. She'd probably imagined it.

EVEN THOUGH THEY HAD no evidence that pointed
directly toward an arrest, Brady wasn't disappointed with their progress thus far. When he
turned the address of Smith's house to the FBI
techs and researchers, he knew they'd come up
with some interesting connections. The sheer
luxury of that house was an indication that serious money was involved.

The route leading to Smith's last stop was
fairly desolate. Unlike the forested approach to
the house, they drove through open terrain with
barbed wire fencing. As far as he could see in the
night, the land was covered with dry brush and
low scrub. If they got too close, their truck would
be noticed.

"It's about two miles from here," he said. "Find
a place to pull over and park."

"There's nowhere to hide the truck."

He pointed. "There's a turnoff."

She drove down a short dirt road to a metal gate fastened with a chain and a lock. He figured this was a field for grazing cattle, but there were no animals in sight. "Back around so we're facing nose out."

"Right," she said, "so we can make a quick getaway."

He hoped a speedy escape wouldn't be necessary. Finding no evidence was preferable to finding danger. "We'll walk from here."

With the truck parked, she climbed out from behind the driver's seat. "I wish I'd eaten more dinner. Did you happen to bring any water?"

"Always prepared." He kept a six-pack of bottled water in the back of the truck for use in just this sort of occasion. He climbed into the bed and grabbed one for her and one for himself.

After they climbed through the barbed-wire fence and started walking in a southeast direction, he considered the preparations he'd made for tonight and admitted to himself that he'd fallen short. At the very least, Petra should be wearing a bulletproof vest. She should also be armed with two extra clips of ammo.

It wasn't like him to be haphazard. Clearly, he was distracted by her. Half his brain was thinking about what was going to happen later tonight, when they were alone in the house. He concentrated on bringing his focus back to the investigation.

Keeping his voice low, he said, "This is another good dropoff point for the traffickers. There's nothing around. No witnesses."

"What happens to these people when they're dropped off?"

"It's like any other type of distribution," he said. "They're delivered to the highest bidder. The lucky ones are used as low-paid or nonpaid fieldworkers or given jobs in factories."

"Why don't they escape?"

"Fear. Not only are they scared of what the traffickers will do to them, but they're also afraid of being picked up by police and tossed in jail."

"No hope," she said.

In the distance, probably a mile away, he saw lights and the shapes of a couple of barn-size buildings. "We should be quiet from here on. Stay low."

He jogged in a crouch toward the lights. They were bright. Floodlights. The compound was lit like a prison yard. What the hell was going on here? He wouldn't be surprised to encounter armed guards, and there could well be surveillance cameras as well. He and Petra needed to stay invisible.

A barbed wire fence marked off the property line about a hundred yards from a barn, a trailer and a low, flat-roofed building. He signaled Petra to halt and they crouched beside a fence post. There were only a few scraggly trees and the ruins of a former ranch house that looked like it had been destroyed in a fire. Five vehicles were parked outside the barn; one was a motor home.

Petra whispered, "Should we take license numbers?"

"No need." He took out his binoculars. "Tomorrow, I'll make sure the FBI has this compound under aerial surveillance."

The barn door was closed and latched. Using the binoculars, he scanned the side entrance. That door was also closed. Anything could be happening inside the barn. It was big enough to hide a semi. Lights inside the trailer were lit, and Brady figured it was being used for living quarters.

He couldn't guess at the function of the low building that looked like it had been constructed recently. There was only one window. The center entrance was a double-wide door.

Two men emerged from the trailer. Their voices carried in the still night, but they were too far away to make out the words. One of them laughed. A young guy, he was wearing a backward baseball cap. When Brady focused in, he saw the guns on their hips. What were they protecting?

The guy with the cap entered the low building

with the double doors. The other went to the vehicles and started up a commercial van that was
painted brown and looked like a delivery truck.

"What are they doing?" Petra whispered.

He signaled for silence and passed her the
binoculars. Starlight shone in her hair, making
him think again of possible surveillance cameras.
They needed to get out of here.

The van pulled up to the building, and the guy
got out. He opened the back of the van, and then
went into the building. They were preparing to
transport something.

Petra handed the binoculars back to him, and he
watched as the double doors were propped open.
The two men came out. Between them, they carried a body bag.

Chapter Seventeen

Petra watched two body bags being loaded into the van. The fate of these victims would never be known. Their families would never be notified. They were just...gone.

All along, Brady had been telling her about the horrors of human trafficking, but it took this visceral, visual experience to make her fully aware. She was shocked. And saddened. And outraged beyond any anger she'd ever felt before. "We've got to stop them."

"Hush."

"We can't let them drive away with those bodies." As soon as that plain delivery van joined in regular traffic, it would never be noticed. The dead would be erased. And the victims deserved more than that. Their passing needed to be recognized and acknowledged.

A third man came out of the trailer. He had a rifle slung across his shoulder. After a brief pause to talk with the other two, he sauntered toward the barn, which was closer to where they were crouched beside the fence post.

"Lie flat," Brady whispered as he stretched out on the ground.

It seemed impossible that the man with the rifle was coming after them. How would he know they were here? *Unless there was a surveillance camera.* Brady had mentioned that possibility when they were at Smith's house. If a camera was hidden on top of the barn, the rifleman could have been sitting in the trailer watching them on a screen. He might know exactly where they were hiding.

She did as Brady ordered and lay down on her belly. The earth beneath her felt cool. It smelled like dust and mildew. Peering through the brush, she could see the man with the rifle coming around the side of the barn. He wasn't far away, less than the length of a football field. She and Brady were within easy range of his rifle.

Beside her, Brady moved cautiously to take his gun from the holster. At this distance, a handgun against a rifle was no contest, not even for the most brilliant marksman on earth. She figured their only advantage was the darkness, and that didn't count for much. Any decent hunting rifle had a night vision scope.

Her muscles tensed, preparing to take off running if Brady gave the signal. She was scared.

Didn't want to be, but couldn't help it. Her fingers closed around her amethyst necklace. If ever she had needed protection, now was the time.

At the side of the barn, the man with the rifle stepped beyond the glare of the floodlights. Even though he was in shadow, she could still see him as he leaned his weapon against the side of the barn, reached into his pocket and took out a pack of cigarettes. If they were lucky, he'd just come outside for a smoke. If not, he was toying with them, choosing his moment before he opened fire.

His lighter flared as he lit up. He was too far away for her to smell the smoke, but her senses were so heightened that she imagined the nicotine scent and wrinkled her nose.

The other two called to the man with the rifle. He picked up his weapon and sauntered back toward the others.

Brady gave her a nudge. "Go. Stay as low as you can."

Crouched nearly double, she ran beside him as he dashed toward a clump of trees. When they made it to that shelter, Brady looked back over his shoulder. She did the same.

All three men were talking and laughing, paying no attention to them.

Brady spoke quietly. "Move fast. We need to get away before that delivery truck sees where we're parked."

Following his lead, she ducked and dodged and ran in a crouch that strained her muscles. Her back prickled as though expecting at any moment to be shot. Were they really safe?

It was a huge relief when they could finally stand upright and run. The wind swept across her cheeks. Her hairline was damp, and she realized that she'd been sweating.

When they got to the truck, her hands were trembling. She handed him the keys. "You drive."

Even though she could have managed to pull the truck around and get back to the house, she needed a chance to catch her breath. The inside of her head was raw confusion. They could have been killed. She and Brady could have been zipped into body bags of their own. What was going on at this secret compound? What was Smith doing?

As soon as Brady drove onto the road, he hit the accelerator. The truck sped through the dark. No headlights.

Acting on pure reflex, she threw her arm out straight to brace herself against the dashboard as the truck careened onto the shoulder of the road. The back end swiveled and swerved.

"Lights," she yelled, "turn on the lights."

"We're okay."

Not really. The truck went flying over a bump. She should have bought new tires. These all-season tires weren't gripping the way they should. "Brady, please."

"I've got everything under control."

Mr. Toad's Wild Ride had nothing on this. "Lights on. Now."

"Fine." He was still speeding, but the truck wasn't plunging into darkness. "Better?"

"Why were you driving like a maniac?"

"Couldn't take a chance on being spotted." His utter calm infuriated her. "Those guys don't know we're on to them, and that is our best advantage."

She glared at his profile. "This truck is my only vehicle. I don't want it wrecked."

He had the nerve to grin. "It almost sounds like you don't trust me."

"Because you don't make any sense, none at all. When I was going to Lost Lamb, you were all nervous about having me in danger. But you dragged me to this compound without even giving me a gun."

"I didn't expect this to be dangerous."

The body bags changed everything. People were being killed. "What are we going to do? You can't let that guy drive away with the bodies. It's not right for those victims to just disappear."

"Agreed. When we get back to the house, I'll make the necessary phone calls. That delivery van will be tracked to its final destination. Where and how they dispose of the bodies is important."

Half to himself, he added, "Too bad the ITEP task force is mostly disbanded. I could use the extra man power."

How could he be so calm? His hands were steady on the steering wheel. His features were relaxed, as though he was thinking of the answer to a clue in the crossword puzzle.

On the other hand, she felt as though she was being buffeted by a wild tornado, swirling through questions that spun into more questions. She wanted to scream, but that wouldn't do much good. She got a grip on her emotions, concentrated on her breathing and tried to settle her mind.

After one more slow exhale, she asked, "What was going on at that compound?"

"It's some kind of dropoff point. That's probably what the barn is used for. It's big enough to hide a semi inside."

"And the building where they kept the dead bodies?"

"Double doors," he said. "What does that suggest?"

"Something large is being moved in and out."

"And Dr. Smith is involved." Brady was still driving too fast for this narrow road. The tires squealed as they rounded a curve. "I'm thinking the wide doors are to accommodate the coming and going of hospital gurneys. That place is some kind of clinic."

"A clinic where the patients don't survive." She was afraid that Brady's logic was correct. Smith was performing operations, possibly some kind of experiment. "Do you think this involves the surrogates?"

"Let's assume that Smith does the artificial insemination process or he supervises it. And he probably uses that building as a lab."

Why would these women be dying? In vitro wasn't considered life-threatening, certainly not dangerous enough to kill two women in a brief period of time. "I can't make sense of what I saw. Two body bags. Two victims."

"I saw more clearly than you did," Brady said. "Remember, I had the night vision binoculars when the bags were brought out. From the shape, I couldn't tell if they were male or female. But the second one was heavy. The two guys carrying it were struggling with the weight. That makes me think it was a man."

"Not a surrogate." She shouldn't have felt relief, but she did. It was her job to help and protect pregnant women.

"There's something more going on than making babies. That clinic or laboratory or whatever the hell you want to call it is being used for something that affects men and women."

"Some kind of weird experimentation?"

"Nothing so exotic."

Brady took a left turn onto a main road. Right away, she saw another truck coming toward them at a safe, sane speed. A sign by the road indicated that they were seven miles from Kirkland. The atmosphere changed from dark and scary into something approaching normal.

Gearing her breathing to a steady rhythm, she willed herself toward a deeper relaxation. Her hands rested in her lap. Consciously, she wiggled her fingers and brushed the tension away. "You seem to have an idea of what's going on."

"I've seen something similar."

She heard an undercurrent of rage in his voice. "You're angry."

"It makes me mad that a psychotic like Smith can stroll around his mansion, exercise on his stationary bike and watch the news on his big-screen TV while his victims are suffering the worst possible outcome of human trafficking. I'm going to stop him, Petra. If it's the last thing I do in this life, I will put an end to this."

His anger was something she could understand, and she preferred it to his cool logic. "What is Smith doing to these people?"

"When they get swept into the human trafficking network, they're chattel. Their experiences and thoughts, even their souls, count for nothing. They're exploited for profit. They're sold."

"Then why would they be killed?"

"Sometimes, they're sold piece by piece. A kidney. A liver. A heart." He shot her a glance. "Smith is harvesting organs from these people to be sold for transplants on the black market."

Although the process was unimaginable, she knew that Brady was correct. Inside that bland little building in the middle of nowhere, Smith was running a sophisticated operation. He had to run tests to make sure the donors were a good match for the end user. Taking a viable organ required a surgeon's skill. Performing these operations on innocent victims meant Dr. Smith was pure evil.

As they drove through Kirkland, she caught sight of a clock in the window of a shop. It wasn't even midnight.

She asked, "Do you have enough evidence to close down the operation?"

"Don't worry. No one else is going to get hurt."

"How can you be sure?"

"Trust me," he said.

She truly did trust him. If anybody could take down this complicated human trafficking operation, it was Brady.

Chapter Eighteen

Back at the house, Petra went upstairs and changed into plaid flannel pajama bottoms and a long-sleeved turquoise T-shirt. She unfastened her ponytail and brushed her hair to get out the dust and twigs she picked up when they were hiding by the fence outside the compound.

Brady was in his studio, talking on the phone and sending messages on his computer. She knew he was activating the full force of FBI surveillance, including choppers and satellites. When she peeked through the door, she saw him scribbling on the sketchpad where they made notes earlier today. It didn't seem like there was anything she could do to help the investigation, so she went down to the kitchen and brewed a couple of mugs of chamomile tea.

Because they hadn't gone grocery shopping, the choice of fresh food was minimal. She put together a midnight snack of toast, peanut butter and bananas—healthy foods that promoted a good night's sleep. Bananas have tryptophan, magnesium and potassium to relax the muscles. And the peanut butter is a source of niacin that helps release serotonin. Good stuff, she arranged it on plates and took it upstairs on a tray.

Bringing him food and standing in the background wasn't the way she'd expected tonight to turn out. Earlier, she and Brady had been on track to make love. Now, she doubted that would happen. The investigation had rocketed into high gear, leaving their potential relationship in the dust.

She glanced down at the wedding band with the Celtic knot design. It was beautiful but meant nothing. They'd been undercover, pretending to be husband and wife. In real life, they weren't connected.

When she placed the plate of food and the tea on the table beside him, he glanced up. For a moment, his gaze tangled with hers. A smile flashed across his face, and his dimple winked at her as he mouthed the words *thank you*.

She gave him a nod and stepped back, watching as he continued his conversations. The first thing he'd done when they got back to the house was to check the bug that he'd planted in Francine's office. Apparently, she didn't spend a whole lot of time behind her desk. There were only a few other conversations, but nothing significant.

Because Brady's art supplies took up every surface in the studio and the only real place to sit was his stool in front of the drafting table, she perched on the windowsill and nibbled as she watched him make his phone calls and coordinate the task force. He was more than competent when it came to organization, as skillful as a maestro conducting an orchestra.

To her surprise, he held the phone toward her. "Cole wants to say hello."

She swallowed a bite of peanut butter and took the phone. "Hey, Cole."

"Rachel says hi. She wanted me to tell you that everything is fine in Granby. No babies to deliver. And she's enjoying the classes with your yoga moms."

The description of Petra's regular life seemed so normal and tame…and boring. "Tell her thanks again for filling in."

"She also wants to know how you and Brady are getting along…" His voice trailed off. "It's none of my business, but Rachel said I should tell you that feds make good husbands."

"Is that so?" Rachel had been happily single into her thirties. After she and Cole got together, she couldn't stand to see anyone else unwed. "Tell her not to order that bridesmaid dress just yet."

"He's a good man, Petra."

"You're as bad as your wife," she said. "Do you want to talk to Brady again?"

"We're done," Cole said. "Sweet dreams."

She disconnected the call and handed the phone back to Brady. "That was weird. Cole and Rachel are playing matchmaker."

"They mean well." He set down the phone and took a gulp of his tea. "They want everybody to be as happy as they are."

"They aren't the only ones," she said. "I'm around these hormonal pregnant women all the time, and they really want me to couple up. They keep fixing me up and introducing me around. Sometimes, I think that if all the guys I've been on blind dates with held hands, they'd circle the globe."

"That's a strange image."

"I've met some strange men. And I'll bet you've had the same experience with blind dates."

"I never kiss and tell."

She finished her sandwich and dabbed at her mouth with a paper towel. "Have you got everything organized?"

"You'll be happy to know that the delivery van with the body bags is under surveillance as we speak. There's an eye in the sky watching the compound, Smith's house and Lost Lamb. The ITEP task force is coordinating backup for when we decide to move in and make arrests."

"You must be happy," she said. "You finally have a plan."

"I'm thinking that we'll wait to make our move until after Francine has her meeting with the lawyer tomorrow afternoon. Cole can make the search at Mancuso's office. And you and I can listen on the bug to what they say. We might pick up a few more bits of evidence."

She crossed the studio and pointed to the number one name on the list they'd made. "What happens to Dee and her baby?"

"They'll be safe. Lost Lamb will be closed down and arrangements will be made for the women."

"This fell together nicely," she said. "After we made all these elaborate preparations to be an undercover husband and wife, the case was solved with a bug and a GPS tracker."

"Which never would have happened if we hadn't gotten inside Lost Lamb." He stood and pulled her into a hug. "You were the key to this whole operation."

Even though his embrace seemed more friendly than sexy, she felt stirrings. Her heart gave an excited little leap. "Yeah, we're a good team."

"We're more than that, Petra. A lot more."

When he squeezed her, it took all her willpower not to respond.

"What's wrong?" he asked.

"Nothing. I'm fine," she said quickly.

He released his embrace. His head tilted to one side as he studied her. "There's a wall between us. Why?"

"It's nothing, Brady. Really, I'm not complaining. We've done great. Our investigation is a success and putting an end to this horror is a hundred times more important than my feelings."

"Not to me," he said. "You know better than to put yourself in second place. You're the queen of positive thinking."

"You're right." She never ever disregarded her feelings.

"What's really going on?"

She inhaled a deep breath and tried to find the truth inside herself. "I'm a little sad. I had thought there might be a relationship between us, but that's not going to happen. You're leaving. I can't let myself get any closer to you and then say goodbye."

"Come with me."

She hesitated. "Where?"

"I want to be alone with you."

"Alone?" What was he talking about? She glanced around the studio. "Is there somebody else in the house?"

"It's all this equipment. I feel like the FBI is in the room with us watching."

He took her hand and led her into his bedroom.

She was about to object, but he didn't stop at the bed. Instead, he opened the door to the balcony and held it for her. She stepped outside into the night.

ON THE CEDAR BALCONY, Brady slipped his arm around her and guided her to the railing. A sliver of moon hung in the night sky and the stars looked down on them. The fresh air brushed his face. "It's a beautiful night."

As she lifted her chin, he admired the slender column of her throat. "A Virgo moon," she said.

"Meaning?"

"I think of September as the time for harvest, to reap what we've sown and take stock."

"I like it," he said. Taking stock was one of his favorite things. "Under this Virgo moon, it's time to figure out where we are and where we're going."

"Let me guess. You want to make a plan."

"I'm not so sure."

He was on the verge of a change in his life. His thinking was, as always, clear and rational. But there was another element, a subtext. Instead of focusing on his career, he wanted a personal life. He wanted Petra.

"Let me start at the beginning."

"Okay."

"When I flew into the airfield in Granby, I

was sick and tired of the ITEP task force and the southwest. I didn't see the sunset or the mountains, didn't care that the aspens had turned gold. My world stopped at the end of my nose. For eight months, I'd been chasing criminals who would never be brought to justice. I was close to burn-out."

"Talk about your negative vibes."

"Then I walked into the clinic and saw you standing on your head upside down." He would never forget that moment. "You made me curious. For the first time in a long time, I wasn't concentrating on my next promotion or how I could impress my next boss. You filled my mind and opened my eyes."

"I did all that with a headstand?"

She was grinning, trying to keep the mood light. And he didn't want to scare her off by turning serious. But he didn't have much time. If all things went according to plan, tomorrow would be the end of their undercover assignment.

"I don't want to leave you." He took her hand. Her fingers were cold, and he brought them to his lips to warm them with a kiss. "We haven't had enough time together."

"But you have to go. You have to take care of business."

"I'll come back. I promise."

Even though she eyed him suspiciously, she

conceded, "You're not a man who breaks his promises."

"I will never hurt you, Petra. I'm not like the other men you've had relationships with."

"I know."

"The truth is…" He hesitated. "This explanation would be easier if we had days and weeks of courtship to move gradually from one step to another."

"It feels like I've known you for a long time," she said. "Because of the fake marriage, we had to get real close, real fast. I've told you things about myself that very few other people know."

He kissed her hand again. "The truth is that I've fallen for you. I like the way you get bent out of shape when I tease you. All your odd beliefs about crystals and burning sage make me want to know you better. You're as beautiful as the night, the sexiest woman I've ever met."

Her eyes widened. "Even in my flannel pajamas?"

"You'd be sexy in a gunnysack."

"I like this," she said. "Keep talking."

"You can say yes to me right now, and we can explore this relationship together. If that means making love, I'm for it. If you want to wait, that's fine."

"It's up to me?"

"If you tell me to leave and never come back,

I'll go," he said. "But know this. I won't give up. I'll keep trying. I'll make plans and map out strategies to get closer to you."

She flashed a seductive grin and wrinkled her nose. "I'd be your next project."

"And we both know how annoying I can be when I'm getting organized." The ball was in her court. He hoped she was willing to take the risk. "Will you give me a chance?"

She glided into his arms. "Make love to me."

PETRA KNEW HE'D BE a good lover. Brady did everything else well, and she was certain that he hadn't ignored those skills. He started slowly, carefully. When they kissed, his tongue explored her mouth, probing and sweeping. His subtle caresses gently teased her toward the next level of excitement.

And then he switched gears, become more demanding, more aggressive. He pinned her against the balcony railing. His thigh separated her legs, and he pressed hard against her. Her neck arched, and her hair fell down her back. It felt like she was suspended in air, floating.

His hands slid under her T-shirt and up her torso. In a moment, her shirt was gone, and the cool night air flowed across her bare breasts. Her amethyst necklace was cold against her skin.

"Beautiful," he murmured as he kissed her lips,

her chin, her throat. He held her wrists against the railing and gazed down at her. "So sexy."

He lowered his head and took his time, tasting her breasts with light kisses and flicks of his tongue. Trembling sensations ripped across the surface of her skin.

She wriggled to get her hands free and yanked at his shirt, wanting to feel his naked chest against hers. When they melted together, she exhaled a groan. This was good, so very good.

Her legs wrapped around him, and she clung to him. He carried her back into the house, and they fell onto his bed together. The rest of their clothing was torn away in a frenzy of passion.

His body was amazing. She glided her hands over his hard muscle and smooth skin. Moonlight through the bedroom window shone on the dark, springy hair that spread across his chest and down his torso. Lying on his back, he lifted her on top of him, yanking her around as though she was light as a pillow.

She fitted her body against him from neck to toe. His hands grasped her behind, holding her in place. Every move she made provoked a response from him.

Her arousal was building to an exquisite level. Tendrils of sensation unfurled inside her and spread from her core to her toes. They rolled together, and he was on top, rising above her on his elbows, and she spread her legs. She wanted him inside her.

"Wait," he said hoarsely.

"What's wrong?"

"Nothing. I'm getting a condom."

"I should have known. You're so organized."

"Prepared," he said.

She teased, "Do you have a full selection? Color-coded in various textures?"

"Not in the mood for jokes."

Neither was she. Even though she could have told him it wasn't necessary and she wasn't likely to get pregnant, she said nothing. Infertility wasn't a topic she wanted to think about, not now.

When he entered her, she abandoned herself to pure instinct, reveling in his strong thrusts. Her pulse raced. She was gasping as she pulled him deeper, giving as good as she got, until they exploded together.

She fell back on the pillows, gasping as residual tremors vibrated through her body. Pure emotion surrounded her with a many-faceted crystal light that multiplied and reflected.

One thing was certain. Making love with Brady had been the right decision.

Chapter Nineteen

Brady launched himself from the bed at the sound of a cell phone ringing. Gray light through the window told him it was dawn. Barefoot and naked, he dashed toward the studio. *Wrong way.* The ring tone was coming from Petra's bedroom.

He flipped the light switch, blinked at the sudden brightness, grabbed the cell from her bedside table and answered with a mumbled hello.

"Brady? Is that you?"

"Margaret." He recognized her simpering voice. "What's up?"

"I guess you are." She giggled. This was one annoying woman.

"Why do you want to talk to Petra?"

"It's Dee. She's in labor. This time she's not faking."

The timing wasn't great. Life would have been easier if Dee had waited until afternoon when the task force would close in on Lost Lamb and the other facility.

Petra appeared in the doorway. Squinting against the light, she stuck out her hand. "Give me the phone."

He passed it to her. She'd thrown on his T-shirt which hung almost to her knees. Her auburn hair fell around her face in tangles. She looked adorable.

Her end of the conversation was mostly nods. She concluded with, "We'll be there in a minute. Brady will drop me off."

She disconnected the call, tossed the phone on the bed and fell against his chest. She groaned. "I don't want to deliver a baby this morning."

"That's good." He snuggled her warm body. "Because I don't want you to go back to Lost Lamb."

"Wanna go back to bed." Her hand slid down his back until she reached his butt and gave a squeeze. "Wanna stay in bed with you."

The thought of making love to her again aroused him. Last night had been pretty spectacular. "And I want you to stay."

"That's not how being a midwife works. Dee needs me. I've got to go."

She disentangled from his embrace, stretched and yawned. Barefoot, she padded toward the dresser by the closet and pulled out a fresh pair of panties—lacy, black and bikini-style. He suppressed a growl of desire. "It might not be safe for you to go there."

"That's not what you said last night. You told me that Dee and the other women would be taken to safety."

That was the plan. *His plan.* No action would be taken until after Cole had a chance to check out Mancuso's paperwork and Brady listened in on Francine's conversation with the lawyer. There was still a possibility of gathering more evidence before they closed down the entire operation.

He glanced at his wrist. Still no watch. That bit of undercover madness ended right now. He needed to keep track of time.

Petra turned toward him, boldly she looked him up and down. "It's a shame I have to say this, but you should get dressed."

He was willing to use his advantage. "What if I stay naked? What if you join me?"

"Not going to happen." She crossed the room. Her fingers ruffled the hair on his chest. "Much as I'd like to make love to you again, we have to go."

He pulled her close, crushed her against his chest and kissed her hard. His blood rushed to his groin. He was more than ready for morning sex. "Pregnant women are real inconvenient."

She tensed. "That's what Smith said."

The mention of Dr. Smith doused his desire like

a bucket of ice water to the face. "You're right. We need to focus."

He left her to get dressed and went into his own bedroom to pull on a pair of jeans and blue work shirt and his boots. He eyeballed the Beretta on the bedside table. Even though he would have felt justified in taking along his firepower, they were still undercover. For a few more hours, he needed to act like Brady Gilliam, but with one difference. Brady Gilliam was going to start wearing a watch.

As he slipped on his watch, he felt like he was reclaiming an important part of himself. He was in control. It was three minutes past seven o'clock.

Stepping onto the landing, he heard Petra in the bathroom, brushing her teeth. Was there time for coffee? He sprinted downstairs, turning on lights as he went. In the kitchen, he loaded the coffee machine, turned it on and hovered beside it as though his presence would make the water drip faster. There was almost half a pot when Petra came down the staircase.

"Three more minutes," he begged.

"And how are we going to carry that coffee in the truck without spilling?"

He opened a cabinet, reached onto a top shelf and took down two travel mugs. "You didn't really think I'd forget something as important as this, did you?"

"You never forget anything. It's part of your charm."

With travel mugs in hand, they went out to the truck. He was driving. This morning, he was not inclined to race along the winding mountain roads. As he drove, he watched the magenta sunrise lighten the skies. "I wouldn't mind living in Colorado."

"But you want to be in the Behavioral Analysis Unit in Quantico." She sipped her coffee. "It's where your career as a profiler is headed."

"That's the good thing about being in the FBI. There's crime everywhere. I could still do profiling in Colorado, and I'm pretty sure Cole could use me."

"So could I," she said.

He had promised her that he wouldn't leave, and he'd meant what he said. In the foreseeable future, they would be together. It wasn't a sacrifice for him; he liked that picture.

"I wouldn't even mind living in Granby." He knew her house was a rental, which meant she wasn't obligated to stay there. "I'd like a ranch house with a bit of land. Maybe get a dog."

"Slow down," she said. "We're just testing the waters in this relationship."

"That's what I'm doing, thinking of possibilities."

"Planning," she said with some exasperation. "You're always planning."

"It's what I do."

And he could easily see them on a small ranch with golden retriever and a couple of kids. His sister would be over the moon. She'd been bugging him for years to settle down. "How many kids do you want? I'm asking because twins run in my family."

"Oh, look, we're already at Lost Lamb." She straightened her shoulders. "Drive past the big house to the back. Dee's already in the birthing suite."

"We need a code word," he said as he drove through the gate. "I don't expect you to run into any trouble. But if you do, call me with the code word."

"Which is?"

"Rachel." She ought to be able to remember her friend's name. "Say something about Rachel, and I'll know you need help."

"And vice versa," she said. "If you want me to get out of here for some reason, call me with a Rachel."

Lights shone through the windows at the back of the main house where the kitchen was. Francine's side was still dark. She probably slept late.

As soon as he parked the truck, Margaret was rushing toward them. Her gaze was aimed directly at him, and she approached his side of the car. Reluctantly, he lowered the window.

"Good morning, Margaret."

"I just wanted to apologize for waking you," she said breathlessly.

"It's not the first time. I'm used to getting calls at weird hours for my midwife wife."

"Midwife wife," she said. "That's funny."

Petra had already gotten out of the truck. She slung her backpack over her shoulder. "Margaret, how's Dee?"

"Complaining, whining and moaning."

"Sounds about right." Petra called out to him, "When are you coming back for your sitting with Francine?"

He checked his wristwatch, a simple act that gave him immense satisfaction. "At one o'clock. That's six hours. You'll be done before that, won't you?"

"You never can tell."

Margaret piped up, "I was in labor for twelve hours. That's not unusual, especially for a first kid."

He didn't like leaving Petra unguarded for that long, and he was glad they had an emergency code word. "Call me if you need anything."

After a cheery wave, she entered the birthing suite.

Brady looked toward Margaret who hovered

nearby. Later today, when arrests were made and Lost Lamb shut down, he wondered how this young woman would fit into the overall scheme. She appeared to be too naive to know what was going on at this place, and she had a young son. Likely, she'd end up as a protected witness in exchange for testimony against Francine.

Her dark eyes explored his face as though sensing trouble. "Is something wrong, Brady? You look unhappy."

"You're very perceptive." He tried to get a read on her. "Why do you think I'm unhappy?"

"It's probably the same reason as everybody else." She shrugged. "You want something you can't have."

"Is that true for you? What do you want?"

"A home." She spoke quickly as thought she'd been waiting for someone to ask just that question. "I want a real home for me and Jeremy. I want him to have a daddy and the kind of life I never had."

"What's stopping you?"

"I'm stuck here with a bunch of pregnant cows. It's impossible to meet guys, except for the jerks who work here."

Brady pointed out, "You could leave."

Her gaze turned furtive. "I'd never make it on my own. Miss Francine takes care of me and my little boy. We're lucky to have a roof over our heads."

Margaret was as loyal as a cocker spaniel. "Do you always do what Francine says?"

"Always." She tried another smile. "She's looking forward to your sitting. You'll bring a canvas with you today, right?"

"Right." That was another task he could undertake at the house while he was waiting for everything else to fall into place. "Have a good day, Margaret."

IF ANYBODY HAD BEEN watching the house, they would have known with a glance that Brady wasn't a struggling artist recently transplanted from San Francisco. His studio had transformed into a war room with a whiteboard to coordinate communication among the various technical and surveillance people.

An FBI chopper was on the way to a private airfield near Durango. The satellite eye-in-the-sky was keeping watch on the various locations. A local agent from the Denver office was following the delivery van with the body bags that appeared to be on the way to Texas.

According to property records, the compound and Smith's house were owned by the same corporation. An initial computer search turned up the names of three individuals who were owners. The scumbag with the gold teeth that they'd arrested in San Diego was one of them. Francine was another.

Brady was beginning to get the idea that she played a major role in the human trafficking operation. Running the supposed home for unwed mothers at Lost Lamb provided her with cover, as well as being an outlet for illegal adoptions and surrogates.

He ran his theory past Cole who was in Durango, waiting for Mancuso to leave his office.

"I'm not sure how she'd win a place at the top of the food chain." Brady had his phone on speaker so he could use both hands to roughly fill in the canvas with Francine's portrait. "Those positions are usually filled by family or by somebody with serious money."

"What do we know about her family?" Cole asked.

"Not much. There's an indication that she had a kid when she was fifteen, but there's nothing more about the child." It was ironic that Francine had once been an unwed mother and now she shamelessly used young women in the same situation. "Her criminal background involved a call girl operation."

"Call girls or hookers?"

"The high-class variety," Brady said. "She was

based in southern California and had a high-profile clientele."

"That could be your connection to human trafficking. She might have been the mistress of one of the bosses."

That connection might be a significant part of their investigation, especially if Francine's lover was high-profile. Brady went to the whiteboard and scribbled a note for the researchers to find Francine's former client list.

He wished Cole good luck on his search of Mancuso's paperwork and returned to the portrait. In his first session with Francine, he'd done pencil sketches and they'd decided on a pose. His next step was translating that sketch into a rough acrylic on canvas.

His art training was minimal. He'd never planned a career in this field and had started doing portraits as an adjunct to psychology. By painting faces, he gained a different perspective for understanding personalities. Working on Francine, he had to be careful to keep her from looking like the heartless woman she was.

Off and on during the morning, he'd been monitoring the bug in her office. Nothing of significance had happened.

Brady set aside his paintbrush, went downstairs for another cup of coffee and sat on the stool beside the drafting table. He listened as Francine welcomed Mancuso into her office.

She wasted no time with chitchat, didn't offer him tea or coffee, didn't inquire after his health. Her tone was that of a boss with an employee. "Did you prepare a contract for the midwife?"

"I did, and it includes a confidentiality agreement so she won't shoot off her mouth around town."

Stan Mancuso—who Brady assumed would be known as Stan the Man to his friends and associates—had a sour tone to his voice. In his photos, he was unsmiling, which he probably thought would encourage people to take him seriously in spite of a bulbous nose that would have looked appropriate in Clown College.

"You're paranoid," Francine said. "The people in town think we're wonderful for helping these poor, misguided girls."

"It's the names that worry me. If anybody figures out how we're juggling these birth certificates and adoption papers, we'll be—"

"No one cares."

"The surrogate program," he said, "is going very well. We're making good money."

"If you can locate more people who want to use surrogates, I have an idea for how we can pump up the volume."

She outlined a scheme for bypassing the actual

surrogate process, while still charging for the egg donor and the in vitro process. "We'll just use a baby from one of these other girls who show up pregnant."

"But the babies won't have the same DNA as the parents."

Brady found it interesting that the lawyer didn't object to cheating his clients by giving them an infant that wasn't genetically related to them. He and Francine were equally unscrupulous, but Mancuso was more worried that they'd get caught.

"I have a solution," Francine said. "We'll fake the DNA results. I'm sure Dr. Terabian can manage that little task."

"Smith," Mancuso said quickly. "It's Dr. Smith. I don't want my name connected in any way with that man."

"Oh, please." Francine's laugh was cold. "Do you really think you can plausibly deny knowledge of what Terabian is doing?"

"I can try. Fudging the paperwork on adoptions is one thing. What Smith does is another." Mancuso's voice curdled. "It's murder."

A juicy piece of evidence. Brady would turn the name Terabian over to the FBI. Apparently, the doctor had a reputation.

Chapter Twenty

In the birthing suite, Petra had been going through what seemed like an endless labor with Dee. When she'd first arrived, Dee had been ninety percent effaced but only six centimeters dilated with contractions nine minutes apart. Dee hadn't been handling the pain well.

Unlike most of the women Petra worked with, Dee wasn't motivated. She hadn't taken any prenatal classes in breathing techniques or meditation. And she wasn't interested in learning.

Petra had tried to talk to her about breath control, but Dee had given up before they even got started. "Don't tell me what to do," she'd snarled. "I'm the one having this baby. Not you."

She'd also rejected Petra's attempt to act like a cheerleader, giving her the old "rah, rah, you can do it." Dee's response had been to moan even louder.

Petra was doing her best to understand. She knew that the birthing process was hard for Dee.

The woman had no support system whatsoever. Her boyfriend was completely out of the picture, which was probably a good thing because he was the one who offered her up as a surrogate in the first place. There wasn't any family for Dee to lean on, and the closest thing she had to a friend was Margaret who sneered and called her a stupid cow.

On the plus side, Dee was healthy. The fetal monitor showed that her baby had a steady, strong heartbeat. From a purely physical standpoint, this should have been a fairly easy delivery.

The basis for Dee's suffering was emotional. Everybody experiences pain differently, and Dee was so scared that the slightest twinge sent her screaming over the edge. In the nine minutes between contractions, Petra barely had time to calm her down before the pain started again.

Sitting beside Dee on the bed and stroking her forehead, Petra decided to try an off-the-wall distraction. If Dee continued to fight the pain so ferociously, she'd be too exhausted to push when the time came.

As soon as Dee's contraction subsided, Petra said, "Tell me about when you were a star in high school."

"What do you mean?" Dee asked with a whimper.

"You told me that you were the lead in a musical."

"*Oklahoma!* Everybody said I was really good." Her mouth relaxed into a tiny smile. "I liked wearing the costumes and dancing around."

"And the applause," Petra said. "Everybody was applauding for you. Do you remember what that felt like?"

Dee nodded. "I was a star."

"That's the feeling I want you to remember when you have your next contraction. Think of a whole auditorium full of people who are standing and clapping for you."

"Why should I do that?"

"Because it'll take your mind off how much it hurts," Petra said. "And it's kind of true. Right now, you're a star. You are performing a miracle."

"That's right."

Petra left her bedside and adjusted the music she'd brought especially for Dee. Scanning through the show tunes, she found the track for *Oklahoma!* "When the contraction starts, I want you to sing along."

"No way."

"Hey, I'm the midwife here. I know what's best."

Dee clenched her hands into fists. Another contraction was starting.

"Now," Petra said. She turned up the volume. At the top of her lungs, she sang along until Dee finally joined in. Together, they belted out the chorus.

Before the end of the song, the contraction was over.

Dee was breathing hard but not sobbing. "That was better."

"You have a terrific voice. Have you ever thought of singing professionally?"

"Like on one of those reality shows," she said. "I could do that."

The distraction worked. For the next hour, they sang their way through labor. Dee felt good enough to get out of bed and walk around. She waddled into the bathroom, brushed her hair and splashed water on her face.

While they were in the middle of "Seventy-Six Trombones," Margaret entered. Scowling, she folded her arms below her breasts. "What are you two doing?"

"It's a new technique," Petra said. "I call it the Liza Minelli method."

"How much longer is this going to take?" Margaret asked.

"Why do you need to know?"

"There are arrangements to be made. I have to take the baby."

"No, you don't," Dee said. "I'm keeping my son."

Margaret glared at her. "You can't do that, heifer. You signed a contract."

"But I changed my mind."

Petra stepped between the two women. "We'll talk about this later. Right now, Dee needs to concentrate on labor."

"This is your fault." Margaret jabbed her skinny finger in Petra's face. "Before you came here and started filling her head with stupid ideas about the miracle of birth, Dee couldn't wait to get rid of the kid."

"How about a little sympathy," Petra said quietly. "You were once in Dee's position."

"That's different."

"And you kept Jeremy."

"Miss Francine said it was all right. She wanted me to keep him."

"Why?" Petra questioned.

"Because my son is…" Margaret's voice trailed off. "None of your business. I know you're up to something. I'm not sure what it is, but I know."

Had she somehow figured out what was going on? Margaret seemed so ineffectual and naive. Was there a different side to her personality? "Tell me."

"I'm out of here."

Dee groaned. "I want my baby."

"Don't worry." Petra returned to her bedside. "Nothing bad is going to happen to your child."

She continued with the contraction sing-along, but her mind was in a darker place. It sounded like Margaret would take the baby as soon as she cut the umbilical cord, and Petra couldn't allow that to happen. She wouldn't let this baby be hauled into an uncertain future.

How much more time did they have? After the next contraction, she examined Dee. She was at eight centimeters. Hard labor would be starting soon.

Until now, the day had been crawling along. Now, she wanted to stop the clock. She checked the time. It was a little before noon.

Brady was supposed to be here for his sitting with Francine at one. Would it be soon enough? She needed him to be here for backup.

"Just keep singing, Dee. I have to make a phone call."

"Don't leave me alone," she wailed. "I'm having contractions all the time."

"Four minutes apart." She couldn't leave her. "I'm not going anywhere. I'll be right here."

She opened the door to the birthing suite and looked around. Margaret wouldn't help, but there might be one of the other women who could sit with Dee for a few minutes.

At the far edge of the house, she spotted someone on horseback. An iconic Western figure, similar to the silhouette she'd glimpsed last night, he was watching and waiting.

Frantically, she waved her arms and called to him. "Robert, over here. Robert."

The big man rode toward her. "What's the trouble?"

"It's Dee. She's getting close to having her baby."

At the mention of Dee's name, he swung down from the saddle. "I'm kind of dirty."

"She won't care."

Petra ushered him through the door just as Dee started singing about her secret love. Her voice trembled with vulnerability as she continued to sing and to reach toward Robert. Her blue eyes were shining at the verge of tears. She might not have the best voice in the world, but she was quite the little actress.

Robert took one look at her and melted. He crossed the room, enclosed her hand in his huge grasp and knelt beside her bed. "I'm here, Dee. It's all going to be okay."

Petra hoped that was true. She stepped outside and called Brady on her cell. As soon as he answered, she said, "It looks like Dee is going to give birth within the hour. Remember what we said about Rachel. I think Rachel would advise you to be here when that happens."

"Would Rachel say I should come right now?"

The mere sound of his voice took the edge off her panic. Her mind filled with a vision of Brady, strong and calm. He'd have a plan for what should happen.

She knew he'd take care of her and Dee. He wouldn't let anything bad happen. He'd promised. "I need you."

"I'm on my way."

"Not right away," she said. "When you come for your sitting, see me first."

She ended the phone call. *I need him.*

PETRA'S PHONE CALL LIT Brady's fuse. Even though she'd used their code word, she didn't want him there until one o'clock—less than an hour from right now.

It wasn't enough time.

He'd compiled a significant amount of evidence. Research on Terabian indicated that the doctor was already wanted for trafficking in black market organs. His association with Lost Lamb was enough to shut down the place.

If that wasn't enough, Cole's visit to Mancuso's office had produced a double set of books, similar to accounting ledgers. But this paperwork pertained to adoptions. Using a facade of legal birth certificates and adoption papers, Mancuso ran illegal adoptions that amounted to selling the babies.

For the past couple of hours, Brady had used every shred of his organizational skill to arrange for a two-pronged bust. In a simultaneous action, the FBI would take over the compound where Terabian had his clinic and Lost Lamb.

For the assault at the compound, Brady set up a team of FBI agents under the command of the ITEP task force. Because the guards at that location were armed and dangerous, they'd use a military strike. The chopper was on the way.

The arrests at Lost Lamb required more finesse. This was a potential hostage situation; they had to be careful not to let the pregnant women get caught in the cross fire. Brady had assigned Cole to lead the effort. Along with four other men recruited from local law enforcement, Cole would disarm Robert and the other men who worked there. And he would take Francine into custody.

She was the primary target. From the evidence, Brady knew that Francine was running the show. She was the spider at the center of the web.

Brady was waiting for Cole to get here. As soon as he arrived, they'd go over the details. The two-pronged assault would start. But Brady couldn't wait. Petra needed him.

He checked his wristwatch. Six minutes had passed since the last time he looked. He paced through his studio, through the bedroom and onto the balcony overlooking the front of his house.

Last night, he and Petra stood right here, caressed by moonlight, warmed by each other's bodies.

He returned to his studio. His plan of attack was meticulously outlined on the whiteboard. Details were arranged. Possible obstacles were accounted for.

The bug in Francine's office was on. If she had any suspicion of what was happening, he'd know it first. A hell of a lot of good it would do him if he was here while Petra was taken hostage.

Through the transmission from the bug, he heard Margaret complaining, and Francine telling her that she was a disappointment. When this was over, Margaret would be an invaluable source of information if she could be convinced to turn on the woman she called Miss Francine.

Under his bulletproof vest, his skin itched. He was protected, but Petra wasn't. She was at the ranch, caught in the web. Three more minutes ticked by.

Brady placed the call to Cole. "I'm going in. I'm leaving the house right now."

"Hold on," Cole said. "I'm about twelve minutes away from your place."

"It's all arranged. You're in charge."

Brady couldn't wait.

Petra needed him.

As he drove away from the house, he knew that he was behaving in an irresponsible manner. Protecting Petra wasn't his primary objective of these arrests. But it was the only thought in his head. He had to keep her safe.

Even though he was early for his appointment, he knew Francine wouldn't object. He'd stowed the canvas with her portrait in the back of the truck. That picture was his ticket inside. He had managed to turn Francine's cruel, grasping nature into a cold beauty. She'd love it.

As he approached the entrance to Lost Lamb, his phone rang. He answered, "What?"

"I'm at your house," Cole said. "Your plan is clear. I can take it from here."

"Good." Because there wasn't a choice. Brady had to be at Petra's side. "Start when you're ready."

"Take care of her, buddy."

"I will."

The only other time in his life when Brady had allowed his emotions to rule his actions was when he fought back against his abusive father to rescue his sister. It hadn't been the smartest thing to do, but it was necessary.

He had to be sure Petra was all right. She was everything to him.

BRADY DROVE THE TRUCK past the main house toward the birthing suite at the rear. His undercover identity was pretty much blown, but he didn't want to come across as a federal agent on an arrest mission. Still, he clipped his Beretta to his hip.

There was a horse standing outside the room where Petra was delivering Dee. What the hell was that about? As Brady left the truck, he heard music from inside.

Without knocking, he whipped open the door. A strange scene confronted him. Dee was on the bed, halfway sitting up and leaning forward. Robert was behind her, supporting her against his massive chest. And Petra was in position to deliver the baby.

Petra had been working hard, and he could tell. He saw the strain in her features. When she looked up at him, recognition flashed in her eyes. She whispered, "You're here."

"What can I do to help?"

"Good vibes," she said. "Send out good vibes."

If she'd asked him to strip naked and chant, he would have done it. He stepped back and watched as she did her job.

Staring at Dee, Petra said, "I can see the top of his head. You're almost done. One more push."

"I can't," Dee wailed.

Robert's low voice rumbled. "You're doing great. You're going to have this baby."

Brady had seen a baby being born once before. When his sister was in labor, he'd been in the delivery room with her husband. They'd been in a hospital with everything sanitary and sterile, but his sister matched Dee in intensity and strength.

She pushed. And pushed. Petra encouraged her, and she pushed again.

He saw the baby, saw as the infant took his first breath and made a cry that sounded like a hiccup.

As Petra cheered and Dee sobbed, he and Robert stared at each other in amazement. There was no greater miracle. Brady was stunned.

He watched as Petra did her job, cleaning the baby and sucking mucus from the nostrils. Red-faced, the tiny boy squalled. His arms and legs jerked and wiggled. He was perfect.

Petra looked to Robert. "You washed your hands, right?"

"Yes, ma'am."

"Have you ever held a baby before?"

"Yes." Brady was touched when he saw the big man's eyes fill with tears.

"Get over here," Petra said. "Put this blanket over your sleeve and take the baby while I finish up with Dee."

Brady moved to stand beside Robert. In a few minutes, he could be arresting this man, but for right now they were the same. When Petra placed the tiny bundle in Robert's arms, both men stood in awe.

Returning to Dee, Petra kept up a soothing dialogue while she cut the cord and delivered the afterbirth. She was gentle and efficient at the same time. He couldn't help but admire her skill.

Someday, he thought, this might happen for them. He and Petra might become parents. He wanted that for her.

After she cleaned up and got Dee settled on the bed again, Petra took the baby and held him to her breast.

"Be healthy," she whispered into the tiny ear. "Be strong. Be wise."

Brady was overwhelmed with emotions. He could almost see the light from the good vibes she was always talking about. The world was, indeed, a beautiful place.

He gently wrapped his arm around her waist. "You're going to make a great mom."

She shook her head. "This won't happen for me. I can't have children."

Chapter Twenty-One

Alone at the house, Petra locked the front door, climbed the staircase and collapsed on the bed she and Brady had shared last night. She stared up at the ceiling and replayed that terrible moment when she'd told Brady that she wasn't physically capable of giving him a child.

His gaze had turned inward, and his gray eyes had gone blank. There had been no mistaking his shock. After he'd drawn in a sharp intake of breath, he'd tried to reassure her and tell her that it was all right. He'd done his best to cover his disappointment, but she'd seen how he felt. That moment would be forever branded in her memory.

He wanted a normal life with a little ranch house and a couple of acres. He wanted a dog. And babies. He hoped for twins, and she couldn't make any promises.

Everything else that happened at Lost Lamb was a blur. There had been a lot of shouting and police officers with guns. Brady had drawn his Beretta and pointed it at Robert.

"I have to arrest you," he'd said. "I'm sorry."

The big man hadn't resisted. He'd merely shrugged his giant shoulders. "I guess I knew this was coming."

"How much do you know?"

"Francine is running some kind of scam with the babies. She's got that lawyer and the doctor working for her. They aren't decent folks."

"Why didn't you quit?"

"I was going to." He'd looked at Dee and grinned. "Then she showed up, and I couldn't just leave her here."

Lying back on the pillows, Dee had gazed at him with tenderness that surprised Petra. Giving birth just might have been the best thing that had ever happened to the diva. In the space of a few hours, she'd matured. When she'd promised Robert that she'd wait for him, Petra had believed her.

After that, the birthing suite had been invaded by uniformed deputies and patrolmen. As soon as Petra had been certain that Dee, her baby and the other women were safe, she'd left. Cole had arranged for one of the officers to drive her here. Brady had stayed behind.

Their arrests at the Lost Lamb hadn't been an

unqualified success. Two people had escaped—
Francine and Margaret.

Brady had, of course, blamed himself. "Lack of
organization," he'd said to her.

"You'll find them."

"Margaret will turn up. One of the officers is
taking care of her son. I don't think she'll leave
the boy behind."

But Petra hadn't been so sure. She'd seen Margaret's dark side in the way she treated Dee.
Quiet, little Margaret had been willing to turn
over the newborn to some dangerous third party.
A woman like that was capable of just about anything.

Rolling over on the bed, Petra buried her face
in the pillows. She smelled Brady on the sheets.
She remembered their passion and a shiver went
through her. Their lovemaking had been special.
More than passionate, he had touched her in unimaginable ways. *I need him.* Those three little
words had never been part of her vocabulary when
it came to relationships.

She'd always been the caretaker, the one who
made things work. That didn't happen with Brady.
They shared and compromised. Needing him
wasn't a sign of weakness; it was strength. They
were stronger together than apart.

But she couldn't give him the normal life he
wanted. Long ago, she'd made her peace with

not being able to get pregnant. After delivering dozens of babies, Petra was happy with adoption as a viable alternative. She wouldn't mind using a surrogate—not a forced surrogate like Dee who agreed to that contract for all the wrong reasons. Monitored surrogacy through legal channels was a good thing…if Brady agreed.

As she found herself drifting in that more positive direction, the phone rang. It was Brady.

His voice was low and concerned. "How are you doing?"

She wanted to tell him that she hadn't meant to drop that emotional bombshell on him while he was in the midst of an operation. She wished that she could have been more controlled and rational. All she said was, "I'm okay."

"I wanted to give you an update on what happened at the compound we uncovered last night. Our guys closed in. There was a firefight with the guards, but they surrendered pretty quickly. The FBI apprehended Terabian."

"Were you right about him? Was he harvesting organs?"

"Yes."

Brady was terse, and she was pretty sure she didn't want to know the details. "What about the surrogates?"

"Terabian was handling that, too. They found frozen embryos at the compound."

Sadness trickled through her. These two medical procedures—in vitro fertilization and organ transplant—should have been used for good. Instead, they'd been horribly corrupted by Terabian and the human traffickers.

"What about Mancuso?" she asked.

"Under arrest," Brady said. "The only real screwup in both operations was mine. It's my fault that Francine and Margaret escaped."

Because he'd rushed to her side. "You'll find them."

"I know." He paused. "Petra, I want you to know that…"

"Stop," she said. "I don't want to talk about anything important over the phone. I need to see your face."

"I'll be there as soon as I can, probably in an hour or so."

An "I love you" poised on the tip of her tongue, but she held back. Those words should be spoken in person. "Bye, Brady. Be careful."

"You, too."

She inhaled a deep, cleansing breath and slowly exhaled, releasing the tension from her muscles. There were a million things to think about, but this had been an exhausting day and her throat was sore from belting out show tunes. She closed her eyes, intending to rest for just a minute or two.

When she wakened, Petra wasn't sure how long

she'd been asleep. More than a minute, that was for sure. Was she even awake? A sense of dread hung around her. There was a nightmare feel in the air.

She smelled the fire and saw the smoke. Blinking furiously, she tried to clear her vision. This wasn't happening; it couldn't be.

She staggered to her feet. Looking down, she saw the gray tendrils clinging to her legs and whisking across the hardwood floor. On the landing, she spotted the primary source of the fire. Bright orange flames leaped from Brady's studio, reaching toward her with fierce claws. She had to escape. But the staircase was already burning. There was no way down. No way out.

She stood like a statue, terrified and paralyzed. Her thoughts reached out toward Brady, telling him all the things she'd never have a chance to say. *Brady, I love you.* She loved him. She wanted to be with him. *I need you.*

Her worst fear was coming true. Ever since she was a little girl, she'd been scared of the fires her father investigated. When she told him, he'd laughed and said she had nothing to worry about unless she was a witch who'd be burned at the stake. That comment was probably the main reason she'd never fully embraced Wiccan practices.

The floor beneath her boots was steaming. The

heat of the fire in the studio seared her skin. Her lungs were burning from the smoke. She had to escape.

Forcing herself to move, she returned to the bedroom. She and Brady had gone over this before. He'd made a plan, and she knew the balcony was the best way to get out of the house. The moment she stepped outside, she heard a gunshot.

Petra dropped to the floor of the cedar balcony. She heard a loud voice.

"Might as well stay inside," Francine yelled. "You'll be unconscious from the smoke in a few seconds."

Petra coughed. Francine was correct. The smoke was already poisoning her breath. "You won't get away with this."

"That's where you're wrong. This is how I'll get away. The fire will destroy any evidence Brady has against me. Without evidence, I'll claim I didn't know what Mancuso and Terabian were doing."

Through the bedroom door, she could see the fire moving closer, consuming everything in its path. "Let me go. You don't need to kill me."

"That wasn't my intention. You fall under the category of collateral damage. You just happened to be in the wrong place at the wrong time."

Petra scrambled to her knees, and Francine

fired at her again. Petra sank flat. "Let me get out.
We can talk."

"If I see your face, I'll shoot."

The flames crackled like dry laughter. The fire
was coming for her. "Somebody is going to come.
They'll see the smoke."

"September is a bad time of year for wildfires,"
Francine said. "Lots of people will be up here to
respond. The fire department and the volunteers,
they'll be all over the place. Nobody will notice
me slipping away."

Her plan was horrible in its simplicity. She'd
probably get away with it, and there was nothing
Petra could do to stop her. She was trapped by the
flames. *I won't die like this.* She'd rather be shot.

Raising her head, she peered through the railing. At the edge of the driveway leading to their
house, she saw a figure on horseback. It couldn't
be Robert because Brady had arrested him.

Margaret! Quiet, unassuming, little Margaret
had been watching her and Brady. She'd been following them. She'd as much as admitted it.

Margaret raised a rifle to her shoulder and
aimed at Francine. "Drop your gun."

Francine whirled. "What are you doing here?"

"I've come to put an end to you."

"Don't be ridiculous," Francine said. "We can
work together. I've got plenty of money tucked
away in an off-shore account. We'll be fine."

"I'm not like you, Mother."

"Actually, that's true." Francine sounded smug. "You're not like me. You won't be able to pull that trigger."

Francine turned her gun at Margaret. Before she could aim, Petra's truck crashed into the yard. Brady leaped out. Gun in hand, he charged toward Francine. He was so dominant, so fierce that he didn't even have to speak.

The instant Francine saw him, she tossed her weapon to the ground and raised her hands over her head. The officer accompanying Brady kept her in his sights as he approached.

Brady kept coming until he stood directly below her. "Come on, Petra. You've got to climb down."

"I know." The smoke was making her dizzy.

"Move it, or else I'm coming up to get you."

Petra hauled herself upright. With an effort, she slung her leg over the railing. Flames were reaching toward her from inside the house and from below. She let go of the railing and fell into Brady's waiting arm. Holding her close, he carried her away from the fire. "Are you all right?"

"Been better," she said. "You can put me down now."

"Not yet." He kissed her lips, the tip of her nose, her forehead. "I'm never going to let you out of my sight again."

"I'm glad you're here, but why? Did you see the smoke?"

He allowed her feet to drop to the ground but continued to hold her against him. "I felt it."

"Felt what?"

"I knew you were in trouble. It was a pain, a stabbing pain in my heart. And I knew. I could hear you calling me as clearly as if you were on the phone. I had to come for you."

"Like a mind reader."

He frowned. "And if you ever tell anybody we can read each other's mind, I'll deny it."

She remembered thinking of him, reaching for him with her mind and her heart. "I love you."

"And I love you back. Twice as much."

Swallowing hard, she asked the question that might destroy their relationship before it began. "Do you love me even if I can't give you what you want? Even if I can't get pregnant?"

"There are a lot of kids who need awesome parents like us. When the time comes, I'll put together a flowchart of all the options."

"A flowchart?"

"It's the ultimate in family planning."

She should have known that he'd rise to the challenge. He wasn't somebody who turned his back. "Did I mention that I love you?"

"You did, but I like hearing it."

She looked past his shoulder. The officer had

already cuffed Francine and shoved her into the back of Petra's truck. Margaret had dismounted and stood beside her horse.

There was something Petra needed to do. She stepped out of his embrace and walked toward Margaret. "Thanks for what you did."

"I didn't do this for you," she said peevishly. "I don't even like you."

"Well, I appreciate it all the same."

"I had my own reasons."

"Francine is your mother."

"To my regret," Margaret said. "She ignored me for the first eighteen years of my life. When I had Jeremy, she kept me around to be her handmaiden, insisted that I call her Miss Francine. And she was going to do the same to my son, raise him as her servant. I couldn't let that happen."

Brady stepped around Petra to give Margaret a hug. "I'm going to make sure this turns out all right for you and Jeremy."

She looked up at him and grinned. "This wasn't exactly what I wanted from you, Brady, but I'll take it."

An SUV with the sheriff's logo on the side pulled into the driveway. In the distance, Petra heard the siren from a fire truck.

"We should get out of the way," Brady said. "The firefighters need to get through."

She'd be happy to step back and let him take

the leadership position. "Are you going to get everyone organized?"

"Not my job." He ducked his head and kissed her again. "There's only one thing I want to organize."

"What's that?"

"My life with you."

She grinned. "That might take a lot of work."

"I'm up for the challenge."

And so was she.

* * * * *

LARGER-PRINT BOOKS!

GET 2 FREE LARGER-PRINT NOVELS PLUS
2 FREE GIFTS!

◆ Harlequin®

INTRIGUE®

BREATHTAKING ROMANTIC SUSPENSE

YES! Please send me 2 FREE LARGER-PRINT Harlequin Intrigue® novels and my 2 FREE gifts (gifts are worth about $10). After receiving them, if I don't wish to receive any more books, I can return the shipping statement marked "cancel." If I don't cancel, I will receive 6 brand-new novels every month and be billed just $5.24 per book in the U.S. or $5.99 per book in Canada. That's a saving of at least 13% off the cover price! It's quite a bargain! Shipping and handling is just 50¢ per book in the U.S. and 75¢ per book in Canada.* I understand that accepting the 2 free books and gifts places me under no obligation to buy anything. I can always return a shipment and cancel at any time. Even if I never buy another book, the two free books and gifts are mine to keep forever.

199/399 HDN FERE

Name _____ (PLEASE PRINT)

Address _____ Apt. #

City _____ State/Prov. _____ Zip/Postal Code

Signature (if under 18, a parent or guardian must sign)

Mail to the **Reader Service:**
IN U.S.A.: P.O. Box 1867, Buffalo, NY 14240-1867
IN CANADA: P.O. Box 609, Fort Erie, Ontario L2A 5X3

Not valid for current subscribers to Harlequin Intrigue Larger-Print books.

Are you a subscriber to Harlequin Intrigue books
and want to receive the larger-print edition?
Call 1-800-873-8635 today or visit www.ReaderService.com.

* Terms and prices subject to change without notice. Prices do not include applicable taxes. Sales tax applicable in N.Y. Canadian residents will be charged applicable taxes. Offer not valid in Quebec. This offer is limited to one order per household. All orders subject to credit approval. Credit or debit balances in a customer's account(s) may be offset by any other outstanding balance owed by or to the customer. Please allow 4 to 6 weeks for delivery. Offer available while quantities last.

Your Privacy—The Reader Service is committed to protecting your privacy. Our Privacy Policy is available online at www.ReaderService.com or upon request from the Reader Service.

We make a portion of our mailing list available to reputable third parties that offer products we believe may interest you. If you prefer that we not exchange your name with third parties, or if you wish to clarify or modify your communication preferences, please visit us at www.ReaderService.com/consumerschoice or write to us at Reader Service Preference Service, P.O. Box 9062, Buffalo, NY 14269. Include your complete name and address.

HILP11B